SPLINTERED REALM SERIES

Borrowed Magic: Book .5
Borrowed Amulet: Book 1
Borrowed Chaos: Book 2

BORROWED MAGIC
SPLINTERED REALMS SERIES PREQUEL

JILLEEN DOLBEARE

ICE RAVEN
PUBLICATIONS

CONTENTS

Chapter 1	1
Chapter 2	7
Chapter 3	17
Chapter 4	29
Chapter 5	33
Chapter 6	39
Chapter 7	45
Chapter 8	53
Chapter 9	59
Chapter 10	65
Chapter 11	69
Chapter 12	77
Chapter 13	85
Please Review Borrowed Magic	91
Borrowed Magic	93
About the Author	99
Also by Jilleen Dolbeare	101

Borrowed Magic
Jilleen Dolbeare

Copyright © 2024
Editor: Cissell Ink
Cover Designer: Crimson Phoenix Creations

All rights reserved. No part of this book may be reproduced, scanned, or distributed in any form including digital, electronic, or mechanical, including photocopying, recording, uploading, or by any information storage and retrieval system without prior written consent of the author except for brief quotes for use in reviews.

CHAPTER ONE

My red dragon, Goch, folded his wings and dove. The thrill of the hunt surged through me like lava. The warm wind screamed through my hair as I clung low to his back. The sun beat down on us, the burning fields below adding to the heat. The unicorn we were hunting—its black flames on full display—left fiery hoof tracks behind, ravaging the grasslands as it tried to escape. It gave a loud whinny, calling to the herd, but we'd effectively cut the blasted beasts off.

Unicorns ate meat, and they preferred the young and innocent. That's why most of the governments in the splinters always put them on the bounty list. This one was no exception.

Goch swooped; and just before we hit the dirt, his wings snapped open above the unicorn's back. I leaned over Goch's shoulder; and with a single swing of my sword, I cut off the unicorn's head. It thumped behind us, rolling in the grass and dirt. We circled around. Goch grabbed the head in his talons with surgical precision and glided over the grass. His wings beat in rhythmic, leathery thuds, the wind of his passage fanning the flames higher. We climbed again—masters of the sky.

We were bounty hunting. It was my new part-time job. I worked full-time at the Splintered Haven Inn—a bed & breakfast for supernaturals—with my best friend Brigid, but that job wasn't enough to keep my mind safe, occupied, off of... I shook my head. I wouldn't think about it.

We had to deliver the horn to the Guild to get paid, then I had to return home for my shift at the inn. Goch set us down away from the fire, it probably wouldn't hurt him, but it wasn't safe for me—although with Excalibur's sheath, I'd heal almost instantly.

I'd become the new bearer of Excalibur a year or so ago, but the gift of its enchanted sheath—which granted the owner nearly instant healing—was the icing on the magical sword cake.

I used Excalibur to separate the horn from the head. Then with the crystalline horn in my hand, Goch lifted us into the sky, and we realm walked to Faerie to turn it in.

Realm walking was a magical skill that few races and even fewer individuals possessed, although dragons seemed to be one of the races who did it naturally. Being able to skip along all the realms in the splinters of reality sure made bounty hunting easier.

Goch landed on the roof of the Bounty Hunter's Guild, and I made my way inside and down the stairs to the Guild Master's office. I traded the horn for a hefty silver deposit made directly into my bank account. I was building quite the little nest egg.

Not that I needed it for anything. My other job took care of my monetary needs, and my bestie let me live in her house for free. But I was human, unlike those I hung out with lately, and someday I'd want to give up hunting the splinters and working the front desk and retire to a tiny beach house somewhere. So, I was putting away a tidy sum for a rainy day—even if the money was in another realm.

I climbed back aboard Goch, and we realm walked back to Kilchis, Oregon in the blink of an eye. I was even five minutes early. Go me.

As always, entering the house was like walking into the depths of despair. Everywhere reminded me of Luke. My Luke. My werewolf. My throat closed off whenever I thought of him, and my chest ached. It had been a year, and still the grief was tangible. A thing I couldn't shake off or put away for later unless I was flying or *doing* something.

I opened the back door and stepped into the kitchen. Brigid was sitting at the old oak table, talking to Merlin. Yeah, that Merlin. Merlin the enchanter. Merlin from the stories about King Arthur. Merlin the *gigantic ass*.

They both looked up at me and went silent, the first clue that they'd been talking about me. Brigid gave Merlin a look.

He cleared his throat. "Megan, I need your dragon-riding skills."

Brigid was oblivious, since Merlin was "helping" her learn enchanting, but he had zero manners. A "please" never hurt anyone did it? What with the other horrible things he'd said to me, I had absolutely no desire to do *anything* for him.

"Why? You have a dragon you can ride," I said and turned my back on him. He did have a dragon; he and Goch's grandsire were a riding pair.

"I do, and we'll need him as well."

I looked back at Merlin.

"The Alaskan dragon clan has called in our favors."

My back stiffened. "What favors?"

He looked away.

Son of a bitch. He'd been instrumental in obtaining Excalibur's sheath from the clan, although Goch had brought it to me. What had Merlin done now?

I stared daggers at him.

"To get the sheath, I had to promise the dragons a favor—from both of us."

The fury that lit up my belly burned like lava. I was so incandescent with rage; you could have seen my heat signature from space.

"You could have told me when I took the sheath I'd have given it back!"

He shook his head. "No, as a human, and Excalibur's bearer, you need the protection. One little favor was worth it."

I closed my eyes and sighed, pushing down my rage. The sheath had healed me several times; it was worth a favor, however, not if it was a favor tied to my enemy. "What's the favor?" I hissed.

"The Golden Collar has been stolen."

I reeled back, shocked. The collar had been created by Merlin. It was a device for storing magic. But it had a dark secret; the device had a enslavement function built into the collar itself. When put on someone, they had to obey the person who'd placed the collar on them, or they were tortured with extreme pain until they obeyed. We'd discovered this when Brigid had briefly borrowed the collar from the dragons. Merlin had turned off the collar—before returning it to the dragons—but the function couldn't be removed. If you knew how, you could reactivate it.

"Who took it?" I asked, my voice tight. Having had the collar used on me before, it was an evil thing to be loosed on the world. My skin crawled at the thought of it.

"I don't know, the dragons want us to come, they'll tell us what they know." He turned back to Brigid, dismissing me.

I didn't want to do anything with the bastard. I opened my mouth to tell him I'd take my chances pissing off the dragons rather than go on a quest with him. My eyes had to be burning a hole through the back of his head. I dropped my gaze; he wasn't even looking at me, so no point.

Part of me wanted to stop detesting him—just let it go—and somewhere deep down, I knew my rage at him was childish. I even knew I was putting my grief for Luke on his head, but I couldn't seem to stop. Thinking about what he'd said after Luke died just amped me up again.

Goch's bugle stopped me. Then, his mental voice erupted into my mind.

Megan, we have a quest! His voice was excited and happy.

Dammit.

Merlin was right; I couldn't let my dragon down—all he'd ever done was help me. I sneered at Merlin's back, seething. I was *stuck* on a mission with my worst enemy.

Part of me wanted to ram Excalibur through his tiny, black heart. Another part of me wanted to curl up in a ball and never get up. I'd been inconsolable at Luke's death. Brigid had tried everything to help me. Nothing worked. I was a ghost, same as Luke.

Then, almost a year after, Merlin had come to me and said, "You've never been good enough for Luke. A human will never be far enough up the evolutionary ladder to be a good mate for a werewolf. It's your fault he's dead."

I would never forget those words—they ran through my brain several times a day. The good, adult part of me wondered if he'd done it to snap me out of my fugue after

Luke's death. It worked. It brought me out of my depression and gave me one purpose, at least. However, I kept coming back to those words, then all rational thought left my head. I wasn't going to forgive him.

Only Brigid and Goch had really helped me. I'd go on this quest for Goch and the dragons only. Merlin the crappy enchanter could rot.

I looked at him again and shook my head. He wouldn't change. He would remain who he was and probably had always been. An utter bastard. I'd *die* on that hill.

CHAPTER TWO

I settled in for my shift at the inn. Goch and I planned to go talk to the dragons after my shift. As I settled behind the front desk, relieving Madison Whelan, Luke's sister, I reflected on how strange my life had become. Less than two years ago, I was just an ordinary human in a job I could barely tolerate. Thinking anything like dragons, griffins, or magic existed was just so much fiction.

I'd worked for my bestie, Brigid, before her divorce, then I continued on for her piece-of-crap ex afterward. I'd been meaning to leave the job but hadn't found anything suitable until Brigid had called me, desperate and hurting. That gave me the courage to tell her ex to shove off. I packed a few things, sold the rest, and moved to Oregon.

It was pretty freeing.

I'd moved into the Secret Haven Inn before the idea for the inn had existed. And it was here Brigid told me that magic existed. Since then, I'd met all kinds of magical creatures, been to other realms, and become a dragon rider. Best of all, I'd met my Luke.

Thinking of Luke was crippling. My stomach ached, and

I clutched it, bending over my arm. I took a few deep breaths, then shoved my memories and my grief back down. I shook my head and looked at the list of check-ins that were arriving today. We had a Fae lord—not one I knew—a shifter—the notes didn't include the species—and a ghost whisperer, whatever that was.

Brigid had been a little wary about the ghost whisperer, but she'd interviewed that guest, trying to ensure we didn't have another dumbass who'd set a poltergeist loose in the inn. The cleanup after the last one had been horrendous. And the only ghostbuster we had to call was Luke's very odd aunt—at least she'd been as fun as Dr. Peter Venkman and about as professional.

I straightened up the workspace, arranged everything the way I preferred it, and sat down on the padded stool. Immediately, I had a phone call. A new booking. I added them to the schedule and moved to the next call. Luckily, business had been good. The calls and out-of-realm messages had been steady. We were nearly all booked up for the rest of the year. Job security, I supposed.

I was growing restless. Now that things had stabilized for Brigid, I wondered if it was time to move on. She had her new husband, Gabe, and the Inn. Also, there were no more witches or vampires trying to kill her or steal her magic. But she was my best friend, and I didn't know if I was ready, yet.

The first guest walked in, and I stood up and said my welcome spiel, "Welcome to the Secret Haven Inn, how can I help you?"

The guest looked at me haughtily. With his combined luminous eyes and smooth skin, I realized this was probably the Fae lord.

He approached the desk with a sneer. "You may call me Lord Seamus of Spring Ardath."

I gave him a flat look. He didn't have an entourage, so Spring Ardath mustn't be very large or important. He was also a guest, and he needed to know how things worked while he was here on Earth. This was the usual problem with lords and ladies—their unrealistic expectations of Earth society, particularly in America. Best I nip this in the bud as I'd done with other Fae lords and ladies.

"Look, Seamus, I'm going to give you the lowdown on how to act when you're here. No one is going to call you 'my lord.' You are on vacation, use this time to relax and ignore all the court nonsense you engage in on Faerie. Here, the most formal we get is Mr. Spring or Mr. Ardath. Most of us will call you Seamus if you prefer, or whatever you want to go by."

"I wish to go by Lord Seamus of Spring Ardath."

I stared at him a moment longer, sighed, and texted Brigid. *Got a stubborn one.*

She was upstairs in the attic, and I heard her clomp down the stairs. I thought, *you're in for it now,* but I smiled at him like I would for a small, simple child.

Brigid rounded the post of the stairs and approached the desk. The stubborn lord didn't look at her and continued to glare at me.

"Lordy here won't follow the rules," I said simply.

Brigid cleared her throat so he'd glance at her. He didn't.

"Excuse me, sir," she said nicely.

He finally deigned to look down on her from his impressive height. I could still see most of his face and his frown when he noticed she wasn't human.

"I'm Brigid; I own this establishment. I'm also the great-granddaughter of the King's Pendragon."

And that usually did it for the stubborn ones. This one just frowned deeper. *Oh goody, a Fae high in stubbornness, and no doubt, low in intelligence.* I made a mental note to avoid him as much as possible for the duration of his stay. This guy had Brigid written all over him. She had far more patience than I did.

"Since you are here on our world, we ask that you follow the few guidelines we give." She handed him a sheet of paper, neatly translated into the language of the high Fae.

Running an interrealm inn would have been really tricky without my alexandrite necklace. Brigid had enchanted it so that I could understand all languages. I assumed all visitors had their own universal translator as well. I didn't go anywhere without mine, but we translated documents into the language of the guest if we knew it ahead of time. The Fae usually had a stack of translated docs. They tended to be far more stubborn than guests from other realms.

Brigid continued, "I'm sure someone of your vaunted rank and intelligence can understand the reasons behind these simple rules. Please, do let me know the name by which you wish to be known, and we can proceed. Once you're all paid up, Megan can show you to your room so your vacation can begin."

He puffed out his chest as he nodded graciously at Brigid. Whaddya know, flattery does work. Shame my ability to blow hot air up people's asses was about the same as my ability to fly without a dragon.

He scanned the paper, and I wondered if he'd leave in a

huff. Instead, he glared at me again. "I wish to be called Seamus."

Now, being Fae, all of us knew that wasn't his real name, but part of the title he took when he became lord of whatever place Spring Ardath was. Fae rarely gave you their real names. Names were power.

"Fine, Seamus, sign here."

He did, and then he handed me three bars of Fae silver. I placed it in the safe at my feet, grabbed the keycard for his door, and had him follow me. People from off world rarely knew how to use a keycard or an elevator, so part of me taking him to his room was to show him how to operate both.

He smiled in wonder at the automatic door of the elevator. "Is this magic?"

"Nope, just earth technology."

He nodded, although I doubted he knew the word technology. Presumably, *his* universal translator supplied him with an appropriately synonymous term. Once he was settled in his room, I returned to my position at the front desk.

After that, the other two lodgers showed up quickly. The first was the shifter, but he wasn't alone. He had a woman with him. He hadn't mentioned that previously, but we priced based on dual occupancy, so it didn't really matter. I just had her add her name to his room. After working here and discovering the need to know what kind of supernaturals were staying, I asked her point blank what she was.

She looked at her companion for a beat. He nodded, and she turned to me and confirmed, "I'm a deer shifter."

I made a note for Brigid, to warn the other guests that deer was off limits for hunting while the deer shifter was here, and I looked at her with interest; I'd never met one before. I smiled, handed them the key card, and directed them to the elevator. They were from the US, so I didn't need to show them how the elevators worked. Which was good, because Seamus was back, pressing the door's open and close buttons in astonishment. The shifters stepped into the elevator, and Seamus took the opportunity to ride up again. I thought about interceding, but I was pretty sure the shifter male could handle it. He gave off alpha vibes and offering to help him would cause a ruckus.

The ghost whisperer arrived soon after. She was very timid and had a Southern accent. She filled out everything, and since I was nosey, I asked her what a ghost whisperer was.

She smiled shyly. "I can see and talk to ghosts."

"Is that something you enjoy, or is it scary?" I asked curiously.

She tilted her hand from side to side. "It can be both, depending on the spirit."

"I bet!"

I gave her the keycard and room number and pointed out the elevator to her. All of my guests were here. Now, I could settle down with a book and occasionally answer the phone. I sighed with relief. I was tired. I'd been hunting that unicorn for the better part of a day. To better fall into a deep, dreamless sleep, I'd been burning the candle at both ends. The more tired I was the less time I spent thinking, remembering.

I pulled out a tattered paperback. It was one of my favorite comfort reads, Anne McCaffrey's *The White Dragon*. I set the book on the desk and leaned over it with my elbows resting on each side. It was so well loved and the spine so broken that it lay flat. It was probably time to get a new copy, but it was like a soft, broken-in pair of jeans. I just didn't want to give it up. They could bury it with me—which might be sooner than later if I didn't stop my current rash of reckless behavior. I wasn't *consciously* trying to join Luke, but...

I focused on the pages, grasping the escapism they offered with both hands. I read until I was rudely interrupted by my nemesis. I turned my book over and glared at him.

"We should leave within the hour," Merlin demanded haughtily.

I looked up at him. He was average height, maybe five-nine or so, and had thick brown hair done stylishly. Unfortunately, he was very handsome—if you liked stuck-up enchanters. The worst thing about him and the best, were his bright, almost too bright, green eyes. It was part of why I hated to look at him. Luke had green eyes... I tore my gaze away.

I placed my hand back on my book. Another person might give him points for being direct. In another life, that person would have been me. I hated time wasters. But then, I hated Merlin more.

"I'm working," I spat out sourly.

He looked at the book pointedly.

I lifted it up to block his face from my vision and continued reading.

He pushed the top of the book down with a single finger.

I lifted it back up.

He harrumphed. "I can do this all day," he promised darkly, pushing my book down again. Bastard. He was a *monster*, but he wasn't going to let me read in peace—and besides, Goch wanted to see the dragons, and I owed them, apparently.

I put the book down with an annoyed sigh. "Fine." I swung off the stool and stood.

"I do hate to interrupt your perusal of the classics."

I checked his face to see if he was being sarcastic. His tone sounded that way, but his face was serious. He was hard to read. Probably because he'd been around for like a *million* years and had practice.

"You've read the *Dragonriders of Pern*?" I asked, incredulously. I assumed he only read technical manuals, or worse, *wrote* them.

"Of course. I may have contributed some dragon lore to the late great lady herself."

I gaped at him. "You are such a liar."

He gave me his best grin. I'm sure he thought it was a panty-dropper.

Well, it wouldn't drop mine. I'd tug those things up to my armpits.

He raised his eyebrows, wanting me to acknowledge his superiority, I was sure.

Like that would happen.

I whipped out my phone and texted Brigid. She was around somewhere. *Hey, have to go meet with the dragons, it's slow, but can someone watch the desk?*

Instead of texting back, she wandered out of the kitchen. "I'm free. Go on, save the world."

"Ha ha. Just looking into the theft of your favorite piece of jewelry—The Golden Collar of Dumbass," I said spookily, pointing to Merlin.

She laughed, although Merlin stood fuming a few feet away. She covered her mouth and coughed. "Yeah, no way.

You can keep it, well, you can't, but you know what I mean."

I nodded. I did. When I'd worn it for a couple of minutes to test it, she'd ordered me around. I couldn't rip it off fast enough.

She swept her beautiful copper hair away from her face and looked at my book. She marked my spot with a business card and turned the pages to start the story from the beginning. You can't keep a good book down. I looked at Brigid with envy. I wanted to be reading the damn book. Still, duty called, and it was such a demanding bitch.

I followed Merlin out the kitchen to the back. He thankfully kept his mouth shut. He knew by now I could just about bear his company as long as he kept his trap sealed.

Goch waited, the thin end of his tail whipping back and forth with his eagerness. My heart softened and I smiled. I did love dragon riding, and I loved my goofy one hundred and thirty-year-old teenaged dragon friend, too. Goch was the brightest part of my life; and despite everything, I was so damned grateful to have him.

Goch's attention was on the ground, so I looked down to see he was conversing with Mr. Mittens.

Mr. Mittens was Brigid's protector. In this form, he just looked like a huge, fancy, housecat. His cream fur was accented with silvery grey points, and he had two white front mittens. In his other form, he was a four-hundred-pound killing machine, complete with saber-toothed tiger teeth and the disposition to ask questions *later, if at all.*

He turned his head and his brilliant periwinkle blue eyes stared at me with intense intelligence. I smiled at him, too. He'd saved my butt more than once; and trust me, you didn't want to end up on his bad side—that was a sure way to end up dead and on his menu.

Mr. Mittens stood leisurely and walked towards me, his long floofy tail swaying with his walk.

Do be careful, pet. Brigid wouldn't be happy if you died on a foolish quest. His voice sounded in my mind, warm and baritone, so unlike Goch's excited tone.

"You're welcome to come."

He blinked. *Hmpf, I appreciate the offer, but you know that my power is limited away from the land. I will remain and guard here. I will watch for your return.*

I nodded and, because he liked it, I rubbed his head and scratched behind his ears and under his chin. When he was scritched and scratched to his satisfaction, he strolled away. I watched, astonished, as he walked *through* the back door. I blinked. OK, I might have been seeing things. I shook my head; it didn't matter. I had dragons to meet with and an asshole to ignore.

CHAPTER
THREE

Merlin, whose dragon was on hoard duty in Alaska, had to ride with me on Goch to the Queen's cavern. That chapped my hide, too.

The harness was built for two. I'd had it made so Brigid could ride with me, but I was regretting it now. He climbed up first and attached himself to the harness. I slid in front of him. I wished there was a way to avoid touching him, but there wasn't. He was warm; probably the only thing warm about him was his body heat. He was careful to hold onto the harness and not me, so I didn't have to hack off his hands with Excalibur. I'm sure he was grateful.

The worst part of flying was taking off. I'd devised a method to keep from having my neck snapped. I had to lie forward on the dragon, grasping the harness to hold myself down until we were airborne. That hadn't been a problem with Brigid; I didn't mind her body lying over mine for the short time involved. But now, it was Merlin riding behind me.

When he lay over me, I almost couldn't handle the

sensation. His warmth soaked through me. I shivered and flushed.

Goch took two steps, and his muscles bunched beneath me. Then, a powerful spring and we were in the air. Merlin's warmth was gone a few seconds later as he sat up straight—I could breathe again. Goch's steady wing beats lifted us into the air, and we realm-walked to the Fae practice planet, then to the island where Goch's clan lived.

You couldn't just *appear* at the dragon lair. The queen's guards turned a little cranky if you did, so we circled high above and made our way down slowly. The cool air whipped at my long hair, even in its braid, and cooled down the hot flush I definitely *didn't* have. The fluffy clouds looked like cotton, although I knew they would be wet and cold if you tore through them.

Without warning, Goch turned and dropped us through one. I sputtered, and now completely damp, chastised him. "What was that for!"

A dragon laugh filled my head.

"I'll get you for that!" But I smiled. His joy in flying was equal to mine. We both knew I wouldn't do anything.

We banked around the mountain, making sure the dragons saw us so it was safe to continue. Goch bugled his presence before he dove down and swooped into the huge dragon cavern. The first time I'd been here with Brigid, we'd been challenged by some of the queen's attendants. This time we were here at the dragons' behest. Besides, the queen was Goch's mom, Aurora Golden Scales.

We flew through a series caverns to the queen's audience chamber. She was perched on her stone throne. We landed in front of her, Goch prancing in excitement before bowing his head in deference.

We're here, mother. We're ready for the quest! he said.

Now that Goch had stilled for a hot minute, Merlin and I slid off of his back.

Aurora Golden Scales glanced at me, barely acknowledging that I was here to fulfill my favor. Instead, she addressed Merlin, *Merlin, we are so pleased you have answered our call. You have always been a friend to the dragons.* Merlin swept a flowery courtly bow before the queen, and she preened in the face of his sycophantic fawning.

Shoot me now. Not only did Goch and I have to ferry his arrogant ass around, but he was also a celebrity everywhere we went. And just like a celebrity, it was a wonder his neck could hold up his fat swollen head. I rolled my eyes and crossed my arms over my chest. Why didn't the stupid dragons just ask for Brigid? She had as much magic as this joker, and she was a lot more pleasant to be around.

That's right, the stupid favor. They owed Brigid, and me and dickhead owed them.

Oops, in my disdain for my companion, I almost missed the queen's explanation of what happened. I tuned back in, cursing my inattention.

...The collar was gone. The only beings besides those in my nest and yourself that have been here were the griffins, and of course, the Irish dragons.

Great, I sure hope the griffins had nothing to do with it. Griffins were terrifying, and I wanted to stay on their good side. And there were more dragons in the world? I should probably ask Goch more questions about dragons.

I sent a silent question directed to Goch. The lowly human daren't interrupt the queen, but I had questions. *Ask her if she thinks that the Irish dragons took the collar.*

He gave a slight nod. *Mother, do you think that the Irish dragons or the griffins took the collar?*

She gave a slight tilt of her head. *The griffins did not have access to the hoard. There is a possibility that the Irish dragons took it, since they were invited to examine the hoard.*

I smiled inwardly. Yes! No griffins to deal with. Then I frowned. But it meant we had to deal with other dragons. Ones that weren't the dragons I knew, and dragons were *tricky*. They didn't think the way we did, and their customs and culture were also extremely foreign to a human or a Fae. Hopefully, Goch knew how to deal with them, but he was young, maybe too young for an ambassador level mission. I threw a side-eyed glance at Merlin. At least he was old and had dealings with dragons. He'd said he'd helped Anne McCaffrey; it was possible he knew some Irish dragons. Maybe he'd have some value besides making sure my anger was stoked.

Merlin looked constipated. "The Irish dragons aren't very happy with me, Your Majesty."

Freaking of course not. The *one* time he could be helpful, and he's as much help as a one-toothed beaver in a petrified forest. I clenched my teeth. Nothing was going to be easy. If it weren't for Goch, I'd have said no way was I going on this quest. I would sit this one out, thank you very much!

Aurora Golden Scales lowered her head to Merlin, her ivory teeth longer than his torso. She breathed out and a little flicker of smoke drifted from her nostrils. *You are a friend to dragons. Make sure you remain so, enchanter.*

"Of course, your majesty. I'll make sure they are thoroughly investigated." He gave her another courtly bow.

She gazed at both of us; the weight of her stare was staggering. *Darg, Goch's grandsire, and your former companion, has agreed to accompany you; he'll meet you outside the hoard. You have two weeks to recover the Golden Crown.*

I wondered "or what?" but I didn't ask. The threat was implied. I just hoped it was aimed at the dipshit enchanter and not me. Damn. I did not like owing favors.

Goch lowered himself and extended his left leg so we could scramble up to his back. I wondered if Merlin had a riding harness for Darg. The harness made things easier. Sometimes Goch forgot about me being on his back, and the harness kept me from plummeting to my death. Having Excalibur's sheath meant I healed almost instantly, but even it had its limits. I wasn't so sure if it could reassemble me from a bunch of squished Megan bits.

Merlin settled against me once more, and I gritted my teeth. I squeezed Goch's body with my legs to signal that we were ready. Goch leapt up, his massive wings beating steadily as we maneuvered through the cavern and back out. The hoard was in an extinct volcano relatively near the Queen's cavern court. We burst into the air, and Goch climbed. The last time I'd been to the hoard, we'd dove into the volcano from the top. This time, Darg was waiting at the top on the rim.

Like Goch, he was red scaled. Saying Goch was red simply didn't do him justice, it was like saying a red crayon was the same as a red glitter marker. Goch was all shades of red. Each scale was a study in the depths and tints of red. He had a subtle pattern in slightly darker hues that went from his head to his tail. Sort of similar to a diamondback rattlesnake. In the sun, both dragons shone like rubies.

Darg, being old even by dragon standards, had two magnificent horns that swept off his brow and twisted back like those of a wild goat. Poor Goch had the start of two horns, but he'd broken one on an adventure with Mr. Mittens. He'd also gained a scarred face on the same side.

Luckily, he hadn't lost his eye. His "adventures" weren't for the faint of heart. Luckily, my heart was stronger than an ox's. I patted his side with affection.

Darg bugled at Goch, who echoed it. Goch landed alongside his grandsire.

Merlin spoke telepathically to all of us. *I had a new riding harness made. If you have a spot in mind, we can put it on.*

I assume that Darg answered Merlin directly because I didn't hear his reply. Goch simply followed his grandsire. Both turned and jumped off the side of the mountain, freefalling with wings tight against their sides for several hundred feet before snapping them open and soaring over the woods below. My stomach was left behind, but I whooped with joy.

The dragons lived on a small island in Alaska. It was uninhabited, although there was a logging operation along the beach. The dragons hadn't felt threatened by the presence of the humans, and they had no need for wood, so they hadn't driven the humans away in the same way most humans didn't bother with flies.

On the other side of the coin, most humans didn't know that dragons still existed, present company excepted. Goch had said once that dragons had subtle magic, so those who didn't believe, didn't see them. I only remember one human noticing us when we were out for a flight, it was an Air Force pilot, and she'd looked at us with complete astonishment. I waved, and she waved back, and that was that. I sure hoped her career and her sanity survived that one. No doubt her mind had put it down to stress.

We circled down to an unoccupied stretch of beach and set down. Merlin, who wore a backpack, dismounted from Goch. He pulled out a very similar harness. I suspected my dragon had shared where I'd gotten mine. Merlin laid it out as Darg watched with a suspicious eye.

That doesn't appear to be as tough as our last harness, the old dragon said. This time he directed his conversation to all of us.

"All new material. Lighter, more comfortable, and actually stronger," the enchanter answered.

I frowned. He only knew that because of me! Back before I knew he was an ass, I'd had a bit of hero worship going. I'd told him everything about the harness. Now, he wouldn't fly off the back of his dragon and land on his stupid head.

I thought of chastising myself for more childish self-talk, but then I thought back to what he'd said, and my anger rose in my heart like an inferno.

I crossed one leg, letting the other one dangle. I watched with a smirk as he initially tried to put the harness on upside down, then struggled with the attachments. He looked at me once and frowned, but I'd let him figure it out by himself. He was the *mighty* Merlin after all. If he really needed help, he could swallow his pride and ask.

I watched him wrangle the harness for a solid five minutes until he let out a huff. "What am I doing wrong?" he asked after the second time he switched ends on the harness.

"You're breathing," I answered.

He glowered at me. "You are *hilarious*. We'll get the trip done faster if you help with this blasted thing." He spoke through gritted teeth. I loved that I annoyed him as much as he annoyed me. Misery loves company after all.

Since he actually deigned to ask for help albeit without a "please," I sighed and slid down Goch's outstretched leg.

I grabbed the harness. "Fine. This is upside down and

inside out to start." I flipped the harness around and pointed to the top. "Darg, if you can put your left front leg through here."

The dragon followed my instructions. After his legs were in, I showed Merlin how to adjust the fit and fasten the straps that held it tight against the massive red dragon. Look at me, being the bigger person. This shit was personal growth.

Once the harness was on and as secure as I could make it—Brigid would be sad if Merlin did land on his stupid head, after all—Darg pranced up and down the beach flapping his wings lazily. *This is a much superior design,* he announced delightedly. *My wings are free, and I can take deep breaths.*

"Thanks, I designed it with Goch's help," I said. I might be human, but I had some skills and zero issue with accepting credit where it was due.

"Do you know where we're going?" I asked Merlin now that we were all ready to go.

"Yes, Darg will send an image to Goch, and we'll realm walk to Ireland. It's too long of a flight from here otherwise."

I looked at him flatly. I wasn't an idiot. I had a basic idea of geography; I knew Ireland was around four-thousand-three-hundred miles from here. *Obviously,* we couldn't fly all the way to Ireland. Goch was young and strong, but even that flight would tax his abilities and take several days. I narrowed my eyes at Merlin. He shrugged one shoulder like my irritation didn't matter a whit to him.

Luckily, he stopped talking, mounted Darg, and we launched into the sky.

Since we couldn't realm walk to the same realm without an off-realm stopping point, we walked to the Fae practice planet. I called a halt, and we spiraled down to land in a grassy field.

"What?" he asked.

"We aren't ready to go to Ireland yet. How long will we be? What should I pack? Do I need weapons, magic balls?" I crossed my arms.

"We were just going to have a look around."

"Fine, but I don't know anything about Ireland or the Irish dragons. Why don't you start there, since you have a history with them?"

"They aren't like your American friends."

I felt like slapping the snark off of him. Since I thought the American dragons barely tolerated me, that made me a little tense. How bad would the Irish ones be?

"Why are you just bringing this up now and not when we were still in Alaska?" I asked with a little annoyance in my voice.

"Because I didn't want to discuss the issue in front of the other dragons."

"Darg is part of them."

"Darg is special and will understand; I can't promise that for all of them."

"Hmpf," I said, uttering Mr. Mitten's catchphrase.

Darg gave a little puff of smoke in agreement.

"So, the Irish dragons hate you, too?" I asked.

I could feel the sadness in his tone—I wasn't sure if that was because I'd just said I hated him, or because the Irish dragons did—but he answered, simply, "I'm not their favorite half-Fae enchanter."

"Well other than you and Dana..." I paused and realized what he'd said. "Oh, they prefer Dana?"

Dana was Brigid's great-grandfather's mistress of magic and the former "Lady of the Lake" from the Arthur stories. She was also the ultimate enchanter for portable magic—magic that collapsed into marble sized balls for ease of access and transport.

He sighed. "Yeah, and only just barely more. They don't really like two-legged creatures much at all. Lots of history there."

"So, humans and Fae hunted them?"

"It's even more complicated than that."

I cocked my head and looked at him.

"The original Irish dragons weren't winged. They were great wyrms that the Irish called Ollphéisteanna. Back when people believed in dragons and saw them for what they were, they came to believe that dragons were evil and a scourge upon the land. The truth was they were *good* for the land, but their blood is acidic and a few, not all, could breathe fire. So that scared people. And humans and some part-blooded Fae who lived there killed them, ever hear of St. Patrick?"

I blinked a few times in surprise.

"Well, he and the others drove the few left underground to be seen no more."

"So, where did the current Irish dragons come from?" I asked, confused.

"Wales. Most western dragons, these two included, are of Welsh stock. Your Goch's name is simply Welsh for red."

My eyes flew open wide. I didn't know that. That was kind of a cool fact. I patted Goch's neck. *You are the best of all red dragons*, I said to him privately. I could feel his pleasure at that.

"Are there other types besides the Welsh?" I asked.

"Sure, there are a few various western types and eastern types, sea serpents, and other wyrms in other nations."

I nodded. I'd look them up sometime. For people that

no longer believed in dragons, my fellow humans did have a lot of dragon lore.

I scratched my head. "OK, so how do we ease into accusing them of stealing from *our* dragons?"

"We don't. We just go in using stealth mode and steal the collar back."

CHAPTER
FOUR

Goch bugled, and I swore.

"We're going to steal from the Irish dragons? Are you mad?"

Merlin grinned. "Perhaps." Then he waved his hand, and he and Darg disappeared from sight for a few seconds.

I crossed my arms. "I know that trick, but unless you can bend your shadow magic around the two of us, it won't do much good."

I froze. I had an idea. "We need to go to Faerie and find Dana."

Dana, the original Lady of the Lake, had gifted me with Excalibur, a spear, and a shield. They were encased in marble-sized magical balls that would reveal their hidden prize with a few magic words. The dragons had gifted me—with conditions apparently—Excalibur's sheath.

The dragons liked to collect items in their hoard; and since I was Goch's rider and had helped them with the Golden Collar the first time, they'd given the sheath to me with strings attached. I threw another bitter look at Merlin. I didn't do strings.

"Why? I can use active shadow magic," Merlin insisted.

"Because I don't trust you. I trust her. Also, I know that shadow magic wears off if there's a lot of wind. There's no way we can fly for longer than a few seconds before we're seen. Did you think that through?"

"We don't need to be camouflaged when we fly. We'll have the dragons take us in under the cover of night, and you and I will sneak in with shadow magic."

"For all I know, you're planning to leave me behind as dragon food. I'd rather borrow shadow magic of my own."

He looked annoyed.

To be fair, he'd been helpful in the past and hadn't led me to believe he'd abandon me. At least Brigid and Goch's mom would be displeased if he did. He had to have a healthy fear of both.

"No, I am not planning to leave you. However, it is a good idea in case we get separated since you are *only* human." He looked at me a moment more than I was comfortable with.

"What?" I demanded at his lingering gaze.

"What other borrowed magic do you have besides your weapons?"

I kept the marble sized magic in a zippered pocket I'd sewn into all my pants for convenience. I had some others besides my weapons for emergencies.

"I have a couple of fire balls, a few healing balls, and a couple of specialty Dana balls for the very naughty." I shrugged. Those special magic balls deposited their targets in Dana's private torture prison on Faerie. She liked to experiment. Although she was firmly in the morally grey category, she did only torture the truly evil. I liked Dana, but she was scary. The Fae were definitely *not* human. And Dana was only half Fae. Her other half? Kelpie.

Merlin nodded. "You're right. If Dana can help me make some invisibility magic, it would be a nice addition to your collection."

It would. I rarely needed a reason to be invisible. It was handy when we battled the witches and vamps, but it wasn't something I desired to do on a regular basis.

"Let's go," I said.

Goch and I knew the way to Brigid's grandfather's castle on Faerie. So, I told him to go, and we walked.

We appeared over the battlements. The Pendragon's archers raised their bows at us, but recognized Goch and lowered them. I knew the instant Merlin and Darg appeared when the bows snapped up again. I grinned. I should make Merlin sweat, but Darg didn't deserve that. I had Goch bugle that all was well, and they lowered their weapons again. We circled and made sure that both dragons could land on the roof landing area that Lugh Pendragon, Brigid's great-

grandfather, had prepared.

Goch spiraled down and landed lightly. I slid off, and he scooched over for his grandsire. I waited near the entrance to the stairs.

Darg landed. It was a tight squeeze with both dragons, but more than likely, Goch would show his grandsire where to hunt. He was familiar with the area. Sure enough, once Merlin joined me, the two dragons leapt off the roof.

I waved at a few of the guards I knew and started down the stairs. Although I wasn't a relative like Brigid, I'd spent enough time here with her and training with the baincallan —centaur-like Fae creatures that were the king's elite guard—that most of the castle knew me.

I had an open invitation, and Dana liked me, which was not something just anyone could say. She barely tolerated most people, and only Lugh, her master, could command her.

Merlin followed me quietly down the stairs. Once on the floor where Dana's lab was, I turned down the corridor. Most of the time, she could be found in her lab, unless she was on a mission for her lord.

The huge oak door was open, a sign she was in the lab. I peered in, then knocked quietly to get her attention. You didn't want to startle her in the lab. Things tended to go boom if you did.

Her solid black eyes glanced up at me, and her green-tinted face split with a horsey grin.

"Megan, to what do I owe the pleasure of a visit?"

I smiled back. I genuinely liked the kelpie woman and her fierce nature. Plus, there was no nonsense with her, she told it like it was and killed whoever annoyed her. "I wish it was a visit for pleasure, but I'm here because of him." I pointed a thumb over my shoulder just as Merlin came up behind me.

I don't know why, but she also liked Merlin. Go figure. They had ancient history, not romantic, nothing like that, but they'd been involved in ancient adventures with Lugh, the king of Faerie's Pendragon, and King Arthur, Merlin's adopted human son.

She turned her horsey grin on him. "Myrddin, welcome."

He gave her a courtly bow. "My lady."

You could tell that tickled her to no end. I sighed. Heaven save me from asses who thought they were charming.

CHAPTER
FIVE

I lounged against one of Dana's massive lab tables, arms crossed while Merlin and I explained what we wanted her to make.

She looked me over a few times with assessing glances. Once she was done, she snapped out, "Why haven't you asked for shadow balls before?"

I shrugged. "I've never needed any. You know me, I'm more upfront and personal than secretive."

"True." She gave a sharp nod. "How many balls do you require?"

Frankly, I had zero idea. I'd never been to the Irish dragon lair before, and I still didn't have an explanation of what to expect. I looked at Merlin with my eyebrows raised in question.

"A dozen? More if you can do it in a short time. We've only been given two weeks, and we need time to scout out the area and act, leaving at least a two-day buffer. I'm thinking we can give you three days?"

Dana nodded. She pursed her horsey lips, though, and looked concerned. I almost expected her to say, "I'm giving her all she's got, Captain." Though I doubt she'd ever seen Star Trek. Still, I'd seen her do just as many miracles as Scotty. I hid my laugh behind a hand.

"That is a very short amount of time," Dana complained.

Merlin shrugged.

She huffed and added, "You'll have to help if we are to do this in your time limit."

"Of course, my lady."

You had to give him points for ass kissing.

I waited a while longer while they chatted, but it became clear soon enough that I was surplus to requirements.

I wasn't used to sitting on my butt doing nothing all day. Restless energy was creeping along my spine. We were supposed to be hunting down the collar, cooling my heels waiting for magic balls hadn't been on the to-do list. Still, we had the beginnings of a plan, which was better than going in guns blazing and getting ourselves killed.

I left them to their enchanting; they didn't even notice me walk away.

I hadn't brought anything, not knowing when we left I could potentially be gone for two weeks—if it took the full amount of time the dragons had given us. But there was no reason for me to stay in Faerie if those two were going to be working for three days.

I reached out to Goch and left a note for Dana and Merlin so they'd know I left. I wandered out into the hall. Sorcha, one of my baincallan friends, was walking towards me on two legs. I smiled at her.

"How are you, Sorcha?" I asked with genuine feeling.

"You haven't heard?' she responded.

"No, what?"

"I quit the Scáthanna. I'm a mercenary now."

I was stunned. I thought the only way to quit the king's personal guard was to die. But she looked so miserable, I didn't say that. "Wow, you must be the best mercenary this world has ever seen."

Her wary look faded and smile split her face. "I'm very good, but there isn't much work this close to the high king. Do you and Brigid need any help?"

She and a handful of the other baincallan had been lent to Brigid to help with her witch and vampire problem. Sorcha had spent enough time on earth to be addicted not only to the fast pace, but energy drinks and YouTube as well.

I shook my head. "We don't, things are quiet. But I belong to the Bounty Hunter's Guild, why don't get you signed up there? That might be enough work, and if I can find you a dragon, you could expand into the other realms."

Her face lit up. "Thank you, Megan. I think that is a wonderful idea."

"I'd go with you, but I'm supposed to be on shift at the inn, catch up later?"

She smiled and trotted down the hall. I continued up to the roof.

Goch and I realm walked back home to the Secret Haven Inn.

The big Victorian with its classic red, green, and tan paint welcomed me. It always did. However, then I walked in, and my loss hit me like a slug to the stomach. I gave myself one second, then pushed the loss away, shoving it into the box I'd made for it.

I hadn't eaten, so I was pleased to smell Chef Jack's scrumptious buffet offerings. He made a buffet-style supper once a month, and I got lucky. Chef Jack was a weretiger, but better than that, he was brilliant in the kitchen. He could make a simple hamburger taste like ambrosia.

He looked up from garnishing something when I walked in and gave me a warm smile. "The guests are in the dining room and the food is all set out, except for the desserts."

"Those of us who are about to dine, salute you," I said cheekily and gave him a crisp salute.

His hands were full, but he smiled briefly before focusing back on his task.

"Have you seen Brigid?" I asked.

Mr. Mittens was eating his premium supper, that was a sure hint she was around.

"Front desk."

"Thanks!" I stole a tiny pastry from the plate Chef Jack was decorating, and he growled at me. It was our thing, and I gave him a wink before I skipped out of the door and down the hall.

"Hey, Megan!" Brigid looked up at me with questioning eyebrows.

"Busy?" I asked lightly. I'd basically abandoned my shift, and she'd kindly covered it for me "You want me to take over?"

Brigid twisted back and forth on the stool. "Nah, I only just came back. I put up the 'Call This Number' sign and did my own thing. No one called. This is a quiet group, thank God."

I leaned a hip against the desk. "So, no crazy poltergeists or kitsunes flooding the inn?" I asked, only half-joking.

She rolled her eyes. "Next time, they can deal with Mr. Mittens."

I snickered. Mr. Mittens dealt with problems one way and one way only—he ate them.

"How is your quest going? I didn't expect you back so soon?" She signed a paper and shoved it in a file.

"The dragons gave us two weeks to complete their quest."

"What is it with them and two weeks? Is it the only span of time they understand?" she mumbled. They'd given her two weeks to fix the collar the last time we'd had it in our possession.

I shrugged. "Don't know. But I left 'Merlin the Ass' on Faerie..."

She interrupted me. "Please try and forgive him. He's not that bad."

I froze. "You know what he said to me...after Luke?"

She nodded, and love and concern filled her eyes. "Megan, he did it to help you. Under his tough exterior and overinflated ego, he's kind and has a heart of gold. Give him a chance. Forgive him."

I felt a twinge of guilt. She'd told me this from the time I'd first confided his horrid words to her. I did feel some gratitude that he cared enough to draw me out, but at the same time, his words were so heinous and hurtful, and I still *ached*. I shook my head, more a "I can't talk about it right now," than a no. I blithely changed the subject.

"Merlin and Dana are making me some shadow balls so I can make myself invisible. Then we'll be able to sneak into the Irish dragon lair and steal the collar back."

She blinked. I'd probably just given her whiplash. Her empathy welled up in her eyes, but she accepted the change of topic and my need for it. "That's a lot, back up. The Irish dragons stole the Collar?"

"Our dragons think so. If the Irish dragons didn't,

there's no way we'll make the timeline, but they were the only ones with access to the hoard, apparently."

"That makes sense, I guess—the simplest explanation is most likely. So, you went to Faerie?"

"Yeah, saw Dana, and convinced Sorcha to sign up with the Guild." I leaned forward, "She quit the Scáthanna."

"No way!"

"Yeah, after hanging with us, it seems they became too boring."

"God, the king will hate me." Brigid buried her head in her hands.

"Nah, I reckon you're still in his good graces, or your grandfather would be calling you."

She nodded, looking relieved. "You're right. Never mind, I don't have any plans to hang out in Faerie for a while. The king will forget once the gossip dies."

Court drama thrived on gossip, once something new came around Sorcha and her friendship with Brigid would be forgotten soon enough. "That's the spirit. So, who should I call in to pick up my shifts for the next two weeks?"

"I'm sure Madison will, and maybe I'll see if the new girl, Beth, wants some more hours."

We'd found another werewolf girl from Luke's old pack. She was just out of high school, so we hadn't used her much, but I'm sure she'd like the money. "I'll call her."

Brigid nodded. "Go get your supper, I know you must be starving."

She was right. After I called Beth, I moved through the buffet like a black hole.

CHAPTER SIX

Three days later, Merlin showed up right on schedule.

I was covering the desk, since I'd be gone on the quest, when he wandered in. I'd finished the *White Dragon* and was reading *All the Weyrs of Pern*.

He raised an inquisitive eyebrow at my reading material.

"I finished the other one. This is the next one."

"Really?"

I put the book down. Irritated. "Do you have shadow balls?" I asked before my brain connected to my mouth. Once the neurons finally fired, I felt the urge to giggle at my poor phrasing. Not that I gave a single shit about the condition of his balls, shadowy or otherwise.

"I do." He held up a leather bag bulging with Dana's magical balls. "Plus more."

I sat up and leaned forward. "Really? What other goodies did she throw in?"

He dumped the bag carefully on the counter. They

wouldn't do anything without the appropriate word, but as they were round and wanted to roll away, he hastily gathered them together. The last thing we needed was for them to smash prematurely. Everyone hated a premature smash. I stifled another giggle and looked at the haul.

There was an array of different sizes and colors. I picked out the shadow magic ones immediately. They were smoky grey, and the color swirled in different shades and depths. I picked one up. "Shadow?"

"Yes."

I noticed the fire balls, all in hues of red, but there was a handful of new pearlescent marbles I'd never seen before. I pointed to one. "What are those?"

He smiled. "My idea—ice. They will freeze a dragon for three minutes. Might give us enough time to get away, especially with fiery creatures like dragons."

"What about people? How long?"

He looked thoughtful. "A while. I don't really know."

I gathered them all up and put them back in the bag. "When do you want to go?"

"We can wait until morning. You can finish your shift and your book." He looked distracted, so I frowned, took my bag of balls and my book, and settled back in to read.

He turned and headed back towards the kitchen or the backdoor, wherever he planned to go. I watched him leave. As much as I hated his stupid mouth, he had a nice ass. Not that I cared.

I shook my head and looked down. Cool, I'd finish my book then, and tomorrow, the quest was on. I'd pack accordingly.

A while later, Mr. Mittens startled me when he jumped up on the counter, his floof waving and glowing slightly.

You shouldn't allow the enchanter to get under your skin, he said.

I gave him a flat look. "He's an ass." I scratched behind his ears.

That may be true, but he is helpful and kind to Brigid.

"I'll give him the Brigid thing, but he has been despicable to me, and I'm not ready to forgive him for that."

What did he do, pet?

"He didn't *do* anything; he said something I can't forgive him for."

I'll punish him if that is your desire?

My heart warmed. Mr. Mittens was scary. If he wanted to stand up for me, who was I to stop him? Yet at the same time, Merlin was *my* personal hell. He didn't deserve a Splintercat punishment, which probably entailed the loss of a body part. If Mr. Mittens could offer psychological punishment though, I'd have considered it.

"Thank you, Mr. Mittens, you are the best. But I'll have to decline. I'll deal with him myself."

As you wish. With that, he jumped down and wandered down the hall, his magnificent tail vertical and swaying with every step.

I picked up my book and settled in to read. I'd just gotten absorbed in the tale, when someone cleared their throat. I looked up, startled. It was the Fae lord, whatever his name was.

"May I help you?" I asked.

"I seek female companionship for the evening."

I blinked twice. Was he saying what I thought he was saying? "Excuse me?"

He repeated his request.

I think I saw red. I stood up and leaned over the

counter. "Look here, buddy, this is not a brothel. If you want a girlfriend, you find your own and make sure she gives consent."

I peered over his shoulder to see Brigid laughing. She had her hand over her mouth to block any sound, but she either put him up to this or sent him to me after he asked her.

He frowned. "This is a common request for an inn on Faerie."

"Well, it's offensive on earth. When in Rome..." The look of confusion on his face made me aware that particular saying wasn't in the universal translator. "In other words, buddy, you have to behave similarly to the people in the culture you are in. So no, we don't supply 'companionship.'"

He didn't like it, but he left. I rolled my eyes at Brigid. "What was that all about?"

"I told him the same, but I sent him to you for a second opinion. I mostly wanted to see what you'd do." She snickered.

"Thanks for that, Bridge," I said drily. "Well, I doubt he'll be a repeat customer."

"No, but since he's a huge ass, I'm not worried about losing him."

"Yeah, me either."

"The look on your face, when you realized what he was asking! It was priceless."

"Har har." I tucked my hair behind my ears. "For a minute, I thought he was asking *me* to be his 'companion.'"

Brigid sobered. "Damn, I didn't think about that. He might have thought I sent him to you for that purpose." She started laughing again, bent double as the giggles really took hold of her.

"Thanks a lot. I've been a lot of things, but I'm not a hussy."

That made her laugh harder. "Hussy? We're the same age. Where did you drag that word from, the Great Depression?"

"I've got a large and rich vocabulary, I'll have you know." I put my nose in the air and picked up my book. "I read."

Brigid snorted. "I don't know if your vocab increases with the amount of sci-fi and fantasy books you read."

It was my turn to snort, but mine was derisive. "Ha, shows what you know!"

She smiled and gave me a short bow. "I stand corrected, oh queen of the dictionary."

"You'd better, now go away. It's the good part."

"Yes'm." She left.

No one interrupted me until my shift ended, and Madison took over. I finished the book and went upstairs to my beautiful turret room painted in white and seafoam green and packed. I wasn't the kind of girl who needed a lot, so I barely filled my backpack, putting my collection of borrowed magic on top, and went to soak in my tub. It might be my last chance for a while. The tub was glorious —deep and jetted—and I intended to empty my personal hot water tank. I filled the tub as high as I could; and after adding sweet-smelling salts, I sank into it with a sigh of relief.

I was in the best shape of my life. I'd taken up running years ago, but when I added my weapons training and more active lifestyle, I was *rocking* my forties. Unfortunately, I was still over forty, so sometimes a good soak was needed. I sank below the surface, leaving only my nose above water. Pure heaven.

Sometimes, I wished I had magic like Brigid. She could soak under the water with no issues for long periods of time because she had elemental water magic. But I was just a human. Still, I'd integrated well into the magical world. No one had kicked me out yet, anyway. And no one but Merlin had ever even mentioned it.

CHAPTER
SEVEN

The next morning, while I was preparing Goch, I heard a beat of wings. I looked up and spied Darg flying towards us. Since the parking lot behind the inn wasn't that large, I felt a moment's panic for the few vehicles in the lot, but Darg seemed more careful than Goch, who'd once squashed one of Brigid's cars. Merlin and Darg landed next to us with a whump. Naturally, the landing was textbook.

"Are you ready?" Merlin asked.

I waved a hand over my clearly harnessed dragon. "Is that a rhetorical question?" I asked flatly.

He shrugged. "So it seems."

"Do you have a plan?" I asked.

"I do. I've scouted ahead already, so I'll send Goch an image of where we should land. We can realm walk there."

He looked me over. "Are you appropriately dressed for Ireland?"

I looked down at what I wore—my riding clothes were an insulated design based on reading the Dragonriders of

Pern, only with modern earth materials. So, I wondered what his point was.

"I looked up the weather," I said, my tone pugnacious. Was he implying I wasn't prepared for this?

Merlin eyed me. "Well, it's about ten degrees cooler and windy."

"Fine, I'll grab an extra sweater," I huffed.

"There's a good chance we'll have to sneak through some semi-submerged areas, do you have things that will protect you in cold water?"

"*That* is something I needed to know." I didn't own a wet suit or a dry suit, and I certainly didn't just have one with me, I wasn't a diver. That was info I needed to know far in advance. I glared at Merlin. "Now, we'll have to delay setting off," I groused. "I'll need to go shopping for a wetsuit."

He grimaced. "We can't afford a delay. I'll have to enchant something for you. Just remember, it won't be good for anything but water use once I'm done with it."

"Fine." I patted Goch. *I'll be back in a minute. I need to grab some clothes for the jackass to enchant.* I stomped into the house and went upstairs to my bedroom. I grabbed a pair of leggings and a tight athletic top I didn't care about. Then I marched back down. I tossed the clothes up to Merlin. "Will these do?"

He nodded, closed his eyes, and a bright flash around the clothes let me know that he'd enchanted them. I grabbed them when he tossed them back down. They felt weird and slick, but I shoved them on top of the magic balls in my backpack and strapped the pack on Goch's harness.

I climbed onto Goch's back and settled myself expertly into the harness. "Now, I'm ready."

Merlin lay across his dragon. Darg hunched and then

sprang into the air. Once they were out of the way, Goch did the same, and we were aloft. Takeoffs were the worst on dragon back. I lay down and grasped the harness so nothing on me could wobble or fall off—like my head. Once aloft, the ride was smooth and almost hypnotic, if you didn't mind sudden dives. I'd reminded Goch often enough that he warned me now, most of the time.

We realm walked. Once above the practice planet, Merlin sent his mental picture to me and Goch. It was a beach with hills and some soaring cliffs. I didn't know Ireland had cliffs, but I'd never been there, so why would I?

"The caves are close to the ground, so beware. We'll land on the top of the cliffs. Just follow me and Darg once we arrive."

"OK." I replied.

We walked.

Like Merlin had said, the air here was humid, but cooler than Kilchis. I looked down at the surf and cliffs.

Merlin sent me a mental message. *Keep close; I'm going to camouflage us until we land.* It was early morning in Ireland and still mostly dark.

Goch swept in closer to Darg, until they were almost touching wingtips. Merlin raised his hands, and the dark shadow magic wafted out. I could see it, only because of my necklace, but once it lay over us—nothing. It was freaky. Plus, the air kept trying to sweep it away, so Merlin had to sustain a steady flow to maintain our invisibility. It was strange watching the ground approach me through my invisible dragon, but I felt the landing. I'd dismounted often enough that I could do it by memory and feel, and soon my feet were firmly planted on Irish soil. The wind was still strong though, and our dim outlines kept peeping through as Merlin carried on with the shadow magic.

I had no idea how long he could keep us camouflaged. I knew from Brigid talking about it, it was hard without a link to Faerie, since Earth was magic poor. But Ireland had long had tales of the Fae, so maybe there was a big old link hanging around. Also, Merlin had invented the Golden Collar, which was a magic storage reservoir for when you were away from a link, so who knew what kind of other storage devices he had on his person? He'd lived on and off Earth for a very long time.

Once we had our stuff, Merlin dismissed the dragons; they were going to wait on the practice planet until called for. I raised my eyebrows at that. I couldn't contact Goch when he wasn't on the same planet as me, so I had no idea how we'd contact them. Hopefully, Merlin had a solution to this problem, though I feared I was giving the prick too much credit. Once the dragons disappeared, Merlin dropped the shadow magic.

I must have been frowning in concern, because he raised a red ball and showed me. "Communication device," he explained laconically.

"Across the splinters?" I asked in surprise.

"Yes."

The orbs were clearly of Dana's design; she was a smart woman. "Dana?"

"Of course."

I nodded. "So, what's the plan now?" I was annoyed he kept giving me only broad strokes. It was almost like he didn't trust me or something. Well, the feeling was mutual.

"We're going to climb down to the caves."

I put my hands on my hips. "You know, you could tell me these things before we left. If I knew we'd be climbing, I'd have worn my hiking boots, not my trainers."

He waved a dismissive hand at me. "Maghera is a tourist location; there's an easy trail."

"Tourists? How do the dragons stay hidden?"

He shrugged. "The usual way. People don't believe they exist, plus this area is riddled with caves. The dragon cave has a permanent illusion over it, so people don't know it's there."

"A permanent illusion? How is that done?" I was familiar with how Brigid did magic, and a bit of what Dana did, but Brigid had never done anything that could be considered permanent, and if that was possible, couldn't we use shadow magic more efficiently?

"It's dragon magic,' he said vaguely. "It's much easier to make it permanent because the cave is stationary."

"I know that dragons have some magic, but I didn't know they could do something as impressive as that," I said in surprise.

"There used to be a few dragon mages around, but they are rare now, if any still survive."

"Huh. What do we do when we get inside the cave?"

"We have to make it to the rear cavern; that's where their hoard is located."

Great. Hope it wasn't well-defended. Ha. The dragons were totally going to leave the hoard undefended. This would be a total cakewalk. What? A girl could dream.

Merlin turned and walked across the top of the large hill we were on. I followed. It was mainly rock with scattered sand and native grasses along the way. We didn't see any other people walking around, although it was now nearly full morning light.

"I thought you said this was a tourist location?" I asked to break the silence.

"It is, but it's a very large beach, and we're here early and at high tide."

"Why does that matter?"

"Can't explore the caves at high tide."

"Then why are we here?"

He smiled at me. "I said we'd be getting wet."

I was ready to throttle him. I didn't want to be here, and I really didn't want to be here with him.

"Quit with all the secretive shit; I'm not in the mood."

"Are you ever?" he bitched. "We needed to come when no one, including the dragons, would suspect us. That's why. It'll be unpleasant, but we'll not have anyone, human"—he looked me over with disdain—"or dragon, looking for us. It'll be the best time to have a discreet look about."

I huffed out a breath. "Fine, I need to change then."

He shrugged. "There are toilets by the car park."

"Car park?"

"Yes, that's a parking lot to you uneducated Yanks."

I glared. He'd lived in America longer than I'd been alive. Asshole.

The trail wasn't difficult; and after a long walk, we approached the bathrooms. I looked at them. You had to pay to go in.

"Uh, my euros are in my other jeans," I said sarcastically. He could have warned me that I'd have to pay to change my clothes and pee.

He came over and placed a hand over the pay device. The door swung open.

"Aren't we stealing?"

"No choice, I didn't bring my Irish jeans either," he said drily.

I used the facilities and then quickly changed into my enchanted clothes. I sure hoped they were warm enough.

But I shouldn't have worried. The clothes were warm, actually warmer than my riding clothes. Maybe I'd wear them all the way back home as well, depending on how well they held up in water.

As we walked back to the beach, I noticed all the signs warning of dangerous riptides and no swimming.

"Should we even be going into the water?" I pointed to the signs.

I was a strong swimmer, but no one could tame the ocean.

He grunted. "Don't worry. I know the safe path."

"Safe path, are you nuts?"

"You'll see."

I bet I would—from the bottom of the ocean. This was no doubt part of an elaborate scheme to kill me. He could tell Brigid sorrowfully that it was an accident. Well, screw him. I was an excellent swimmer. I checked that my weapons and Excalibur's sheath were in my secret pocket. I added a few shadow, fire, and ice balls as well. I zipped up the inner pocket after double-checking. We stashed our bags in some rocks where they'd stay dry, and I followed Merlin around the edge of the cliffs and into certain doom. Joy.

CHAPTER
EIGHT

We walked far enough that I was about to slap Merlin on the back of the head and sit down on the sand. But then the sands narrowed until the water was touching the edge of the cliffs, and soon enough we were knee-deep. It made the walking more difficult, but Merlin put his finger to his lips and sent me a silent telepathic message.

We're close. It'd be best to take my hand so I can guide you through the illusion. He held it out.

I glared at the proffered hand. He was nuts if he thought I'd touch him.

No, I'll follow you.

He frowned but dropped his hand.

I stayed close so I wouldn't lose him. He took about five steps and vanished straight into the cliff face. I followed. I thought I was exactly in the same spot where he'd walked in, but I hit stone. I felt around but couldn't see or figure out where to go. Finally, a hand came out of the stone. I grabbed it, and a shock ran up my arm. I swore under my breath. Merlin pulled me through.

"You need to know the path to get through," he said when I stumbled into him on the other side.

"You could have just said that," I grouched, even though he kind of had. Whatever. He hadn't been *clear*.

The cave was huge. I had no idea how large the entrance was, but it had to be big enough for a dragon, but the interior? It was large enough for several dragons with wings outstretched. I looked around in astonishment. With torches along the walls, it was light enough to see. Only, the flames were blue, not yellow.

What are the torches burning? I asked telepathically.

He shrugged. *It's dragon magic.*

The water stayed about knee-deep, which was surprising, since we'd walked through a barrier. I shook my head; I'd worry about it later. I kept waiting for the floor to drop away from me. However, we rose as we went, and soon we were out of the water and walking on damp sand.

I kept my eyes open for the Irish dragons, but Merlin remained unconcerned and didn't mention concealing us. Although, we kept to mental communication.

Uh, where are the dragons?

He looked back at me. *They are in the next chamber. They don't really like the wet and move to the back when the tide comes in.*

It was a walk to the end of the first chamber. We must be deep inside of the hill, and my mind wandered to the tales of the deadly people in the hollow hills, and I shivered.

Are you cold? Merlin asked.

I shook my head. *No, just spooked.*

There are strange things in Ireland. Ancient magic.

Since I'd been thinking it, I asked, *Is there a link to Faerie here?*

He looked at me strangely. *The odd things aren't necessarily because of a link to Faerie.*

I didn't say they were. I was just wondering if it was easy to access magic here or not.

He nodded. *Yes, there is more than one. Just about anywhere you find a stone circle, there is a link to Faerie.*

Interesting, so is there one close enough for you to use?

Yes, there is a stone ring in this cave. Dragons are attracted to magic. Don't worry, I'm topped off.

His condescension was almost too much to bear. I just answered simply, *Good.* I was trying to rein in my irritation. Trying to do what Brigid asked and let it go.

We were approaching the end of the cavern, as signified by the constriction of the cavern to an opening that looked narrow enough for only one dragon to pass through at a time.

Once we are closer to the end, I'll cover us in shadow magic, so stay close, Merlin thought to me.

Did he seriously think I was going to wander off in a foreign dragon cave? I didn't want to get eaten.

I could hear the bugling and "dragon speech" as we approached, and Merlin pulled me closer to him so that we wouldn't be spotted approaching. We crept along the wall of the cave until we were at the pinch point between caverns.

OK, from here on out, silence, and keep a shadow ball handy in case we get separated.

I reached into my zippered pocket and found a grey swirly shadow ball. I held it clenched in my fist and nodded that I was ready.

Merlin moved his hand, and the shadow magic fell over us, hiding us from view from each other and hopefully the dragons. Then he grasped my reluctant hand, and we snuck into the dragon cave.

This cave was surprisingly warm. A glowing pile of rocks radiated warmth. The dragons apparently liked it steamy. Sweat trickled down my back—they liked it really warm.

Merlin selected the path with the fewest dragons. I hoped their sense of smell wasn't that keen. I also hoped that this was the last cave before the hoard.

I sent Merlin a mental message. *How many caverns before we get to the hoard?*

After this one.

Yes! We just had to get through the cave with dozens of —if not more—jewel-colored dragons. Easy peasy.

I looked around at them, but I didn't see a golden dragon. *Where's the queen?*

Merlin looked up in astonishment. He hadn't noticed. *Dammit. Let's hope she's out flying and not at the hoard waiting for us.*

Another shiver ran down my spine. Not a good sign.

Halfway through the cavern, an emerald green dragon swooped down from a high perch and skimmed close to the sandy bottom. I gave a startled squeak and hit the ground which pulled Merlin down with me. He landed with an oof.

I rolled over in time to see the dragon looking down at where we were. I'd given us away.

It took him a minute to bank around and come back. He back winged and set down where we'd been seconds before. The sand swirling up clung to my face and hair, and I closed my eyes to keep them from filling with grit. Merlin tugged me behind a boulder, and I ducked down low next to his warmth.

We're going to get eaten, I said to him silently.

He laughed quietly into my mind. *They didn't see us, and I doubt he'll do more than just investigate.*

As I watched, our footprints disappeared. Air magic. One benefit of hanging with a Fae enchanter.

Sure enough, the dragon poked around but didn't notice us. He lost interest soon enough and continued on his way out of the cavern towards the beach. I let out a quiet sigh of relief.

Merlin tugged my hand, and we continued towards the hoard. And maybe a waiting Queen. Eek.

CHAPTER NINE

I peered around the wall dividing the caverns. Light glanced off the gold and jewels contained within. This hoard looked twice or three times larger than Goch's clan's hoard, if that was even possible.

In Goch's hoard, the elders took turns guarding the hoard by sitting around on perches in an extinct volcano. Here, the caverns were on the beach, so there was nowhere to put the cache of coins, raw ore, jewels, and magical items except on the ground, or in this case, in a gigantic magical container, similar to a gigantic glass fishbowl.

What the heck is that? I asked Merlin, silently.

The cause of my falling out with the Irish dragons, he said drily.

I looked sharply at him. *Explain.*

Now's not really the time, is it?

No, I guess not, I conceded the point with a grimace.

The bowl containing the hoard filled the cavern. Along the bottom of the bowl was a ring of standing stones. Merlin's link to Fae magic. Even I could feel the increase of magic through my enchanted necklace.

Around the rim, a good thirty feet above us, perches made a decorative pattern. On each perch sat a jeweled-colored dragon—one of which was gold—the queen. Merlin groaned.

How are we going to find the collar in that massive hoard bowl? I asked after we drew back.

I was going to call it to us, but with the queen there, they'll be on alert. We need her to leave.

So, a distraction?

Exactly.

What about if we have Goch and Darg come for a visit? They must be friendly, or Aurora Golden Scales would never have invited them to view their hoard. Right?

He frowned. *If they come and "visit" and we steal back the collar, it could cause an incident between both clans, resulting in war. It's best they don't know we know, and we just take it back quietly.*

Fine. You got any brilliant ideas?

Yes, I'm going in. I'll levitate myself up to the hoard while keeping my shadow magic and see if it's anywhere visible. At least it's a starting point. They haven't had it long. I hope it's just sitting on top in plain sight.

Fine. I didn't have another idea, and Merlin risking his own neck sounded good to me.

Use your shadow ball, I can't maintain your camouflage and do this at the same time, he instructed curtly.

I took the ball out of my pocket and activated it. I just had to sit still until he returned. I got comfortable and waited.

Since I had nothing to do, I just watched the Irish dragons as they did whatever they did in their home. Some younger, smaller dragons wrestled and played, while older ones watched and intervened if it got too rough. A few napped on their perches. A truly massive red brought in two large cows and dropped them on the sand. A couple of other dragons joined in on the feast.

I stayed quiet and alert. A small strangely colored dragon came into view. It was smaller than Goch, so I assumed it was young. I'd never seen a dragon colored like it before, so I focused on it. It was like my alexandrite pendant, a mix of blues, greens, and purples that shifted in the light. I was mesmerized. That's when I noticed it. It was wearing *the* collar—The Golden Collar of Merlin. A cry caught in my throat before I hastily stifled the noise. I looked around anxiously, but the small squeak hadn't been noticed.

Who would want to control a young dragon? Why would the elders put up with that? Maybe it was particularly naughty? I also had no idea whether it was male or female. I only knew that golds were always female, and reds were always male, but I didn't think color mattered with the other dragons. In fiction, the color often determined sex, but that seemed to only be partially true on Earth. The older male dragons had horns, but it was impossible to tell on the young.

I sent a silent call to Merlin, *I found it, come back.*

He didn't reply.

Damn him. A small niggle of anxiety wormed its way into my gut, despite myself.

I stood slowly and inched my way back to the edge of the cavern that bordered the hoard. Maybe the rock had blocked my call. I tried again.

Merlin, get your ass back here.

He didn't answer, but I had the sense that he heard and understood. I eased back to my spot. I inspected myself; my camouflage was holding. Movement tended to wear it away quicker, so I was trying not to move much. But when I did move, I did it slowly.

The large red dragon shoved a green out of the way to allow the small alexandrite dragon to eat its fill. Maybe it wasn't enslaved. Here's hoping it just liked the look of the collar and *wanted* to wear it. I looked at the other dragons, not a single one wore any adornment besides their glittery, jeweled scales.

It was different though, so maybe it needed more to fit in? I wish I knew something about what the colors meant. I'd be asking Goch as soon as we were together again. He'd told us that golds were queens and reds were generally sought out to be the queen's mate. Other than that, he hadn't said much about the others.

My outline was starting to show when Merlin finally made it back.

It's on that small dragon eating the cow, I said.

I heard his sharp intake of breath.

What's wrong?

That's something I thought I'd never see again.

Well don't leave me hanging, what is it? I asked grumpily.

That is a young dragon mage.

Dragon mage? You said they were rare!

Incredibly rare. I haven't seen one since my son was alive.

So, who'd try to enslave one and why are the other dragons allowing it?

He looked startled. *You think someone has enslaved it?*

I didn't know so I shrugged—even though I knew he couldn't see me. *I assume that's why they took it, why else would the dragon mage be wearing it?*

Merlin grasped my arm. *I only know of one who would do such a thing, and the presence of that big red dragon makes it even more likely. Come on, we have to get out of here.*

Merlin practically dragged me from the cave and back up to the cliff face where he let the camouflage fall.

Now I could see his face, the concern there made me falter. One thing about Merlin, he was all kinds of confident about everything. Seeing him shook up was causing me to feel a bit nauseous.

"Are you going to share with the class?" I demanded, hands on my hips.

"Someone tried this long ago."

"Tried to enslave a dragon mage?"

"He convinced one to follow him, yes."

"Well, who was it, and how long ago?"

"Long ago, during Arthur's reign."

I felt a cold chill travel down my spine. "Who?"

"Medraut, you might know him as Mordred."

CHAPTER
TEN

"Mordred? The freaking villain in all the Arthur tales?"

"That's the one."

I threw up my hands. "Wasn't he Arthur's son or nephew or something?" I paced. "That would make him human, so it can't be him, right?" I asked hopefully.

Merlin shook his head. "No, he wasn't related to Arthur, and he wasn't human."

"Good night, nurse," I said, throwing up my hands. I stopped right in front of him. "You'd better start at the beginning."

He looked at me and looked away. But as reluctant as he seemed to tell the story, he did anyway.

"Medraut, his real Welsh name, was one of Arthur's knights. He was a good one, too. Like me, he had Fae heritage, and with it some magic. Not as much as I did, but he was a dragonrider as well which made up for some of it. That big red brute? That was, or still is, his bonded dragon."

"Shit."

"Yes, shitty indeed." He looked around, and when he

saw we were still alone, gestured for me to join him cross-legged in the grass.

"How did he convince the dragon to be a jerk? I've found Goch to be very clan oriented, even if he ran away for a time?"

Merlin shrugged. "I don't know, maybe he was power hungry as well." Merlin plucked at the grass for a bit, then continued his tale, "Medraut allowed himself to be corrupted by the idea of power. Having magic and a dragon wasn't enough. He wanted the kingdom. He saw how Arthur was constantly fighting for freedom and decided he could do a better job of running things. He not only convinced his own dragon, but he also convinced a dragon mage to assist him. They were the driving force of Arthur's downfall and his death. Mordred, as one of his knights, knew about Excalibur's sheath and arranged to have it stolen. He hired a Fae temptress to seduce him and steal the sheath. When Arthur battled next and was wounded, that was it." His voice caught.

I actually felt bad for the guy. I might not like him, but it was clear he loved his adopted son and still, after this many years, mourned him.

He unabashedly swept away a tear. "Medraut didn't like how I responded," he said with grim satisfaction. "I ruined his plans and set him back at least fifteen hundred years. Well, my actions and all his bad press from all the Arthurian tales. If he is behind this, enslaving a dragon mage is a good starting point and destroying me would be the icing on the cake."

"So, what do we do now? How do we get the collar if it's on a powerful, enslaved, dragon mage?"

He shook his head. "I don't know."

"You made the collar, can't you anti-slave it?"

He looked away. "Medraut is using my own enchantments against me. He's probably laughing wherever he is."

Merlin was clenching and unclenching his hands, his jaw tight. Dark emotions stormed across his face. We weren't getting anywhere until Merlin got his shit together.

I clapped my hands in front of his face. "Hey, you're the big bad enchanter, and you have what? Like, eleven elements at your command? Snap out of it."

He looked down at his clenched hands and released them. He shook his head, and his shoulders slumped. "He's won. After all this time, he's finally found a way to defeat Arthur. And me, too."

I didn't see how he'd jumped directly to this conclusion. But until he got it together, I wouldn't know. I waited a few more moments. He wasn't snapping out of it. So, I slapped him. His head snapped around as my open hand made contact with his sallow skin. The sound of the hit was deeply satisfying as was the whole experience. My hand stung, but I hoped I'd get another chance to slap the dumbass.

Merlin stared at me in surprise. I was human, but I wasn't a lightweight. That slap had to have hurt; my hand still throbbed.

"Stop. This isn't fifteen hundred years ago, Arthur is gone, and it's just you and Mordred. He can't hurt you anymore. That dragon mage is a child, it can't be as powerful as the adult one he turned long ago."

He blinked a few times, and I saw when his brain re-engaged. "Right. I can't deactivate the slave function while it's on the dragon. It'll take the kid's head off. We have to take it off the mage, first."

"I thought the person who put it on had to take it off?"

"That is true, but I can also take it off. Wouldn't be much of an artifact without a backdoor, right?"

I smiled. "Right." Merlin, the first computer hacker, who'd a thunk? "OK, that's a start. First, we'll lure away Big Red. How far away from the one controlling the collar before it stops working?" I thought a moment more. "More importantly where is Mordred?"

"Very good questions. The collar does have a range. The slaver has to be within a hundred yards to actively use it. We need to determine if Big Red, as you've named him, is the slaver or if it's Medraut himself. I guess we need to go back in."

"I'm pretty sure Big Red is the slaver. I watched him command the dragon mage to eat. The kid was trying to hide."

"Well, that's good, I suppose. One thing crossed off the list. Only, Big Red is inside where he can command the power of the mage." He stopped talking and looked away, thinking.

"How does a dragon mage compare to a Fae one?" I asked.

"Well, the last one far outstripped my abilities, but they can connect to the Earth herself. I cannot. However, we are on a link to Faerie, and Faerie is much richer in magic."

"And that mage is a kid."

"Yes."

I reached into my pocket. "I have this as well." I held up an ice ball.

"Ah, yes, three minutes of frozen dragon. Unfortunately, there are more dragons in that cave than you have ice balls."

"Yeah, but isn't ice one of your elements?"

He smirked suddenly "It is indeed."

CHAPTER
ELEVEN

The tide was heading out by the time we made it back down to the beach. That wasn't good. It meant the tourists would be heading in, and the dragons would be moving back into the first cavern. We needed that spot to prepare our assault.

The undertow was fierce, and I stumbled a few times, fighting it as we pushed our way through the water to the first of the dragon caverns. This time, I had no problem entering through the illusion because I knew without a doubt that it was there. No hand holding required. Thank God.

The cavern was still partially flooded, although the water had receded quite a lot. However, it was wet enough that the dragons hadn't returned to this spot yet. The chill of the cavern and the icy water, regardless of my cozy enchanted athletic wear, made me shiver. It could have been fear, but I'll claim it was the cold.

We climbed up the gentle slope of the cavern, and soon we were out of the water. We advanced along the wall, out of view of the second cavern, as we'd done before. When

Merlin finally found a spot he deemed appropriate, I took out my ice balls and readied them for a throw. I nodded, and Merlin covered us in shadow magic. We crept forward, well, presumably we did, I couldn't see Merlin.

It was my job to freeze Big Red and the dragon mage. Merlin was going to handle the others and grab the collar, then we'd run away. Straight forward plan, no one could screw it up, right?

As I cocked my arm back to throw, a man appeared out of thin air.

Mordred, Merlin snarled in my mind.

Uh oh. The shit was about to hit the fan. Given that he'd popped up out of thin air, it seemed like Mordred had his own shadow magic. That wasn't the extent of his powers either. He waved a causal hand, and a savage windstorm rose up and barreled towards us, effortlessly tearing away our camouflage. Great.

"Merlin, I wondered when you'd show up. You kept me waiting, old boy." He smiled a smile that held no warmth, and a shiver ran down my spine. He had crazy eyes. As much as I hated Merlin, better the devil you know and all that.

Despite the crazy eyes, Mordred was an undeniably handsome man. Maybe six-foot tall, black hair, glittery dark eyes, and an olive complexion. Maybe he was the descendent of a Roman legionnaire, and that's how he'd ended up as a knight of the roundtable. I wasn't going to ask though.

He looked me over and dismissed me with disdain. "You've always enjoyed your human pets, though I don't know why. They are so fragile."

I resisted the urge to meow loudly and back away, leaving the boys to it. Before I could make any kind of a move, a blast of air slammed into me, tossing me into the cave wall. I hit the rock with a crack. The air left my lungs, and my spine and ribs cracked and broke. I slid down the wall. Thanks to the magical sheath in my pocket, the bones knit together almost instantly, but it was excruciating as it did so. I lay unmoving on the cave floor. Frankly, I couldn't move for a minute as every nerve screamed at me.

Mordred turned his back on me and faced Merlin again. He might be able to tell I was human, but he didn't know I carried Excalibur or its sheath, and I didn't want to give that away. I made myself remain still and waited for my chance.

Big Red and the dragon mage now stood by Mordred. I knew that Merlin could take Mordred, he had before. I didn't know how many elements Mordred commanded, but Merlin had eleven. In the Fae world, that meant Merlin was a strong as the high king who was supposed to have the most elements of any Fae. I knew that Brigid and Lugh, her great-grandfather, had more, but it wasn't common knowledge. Mordred had fewer elements, he had to, but with the dragon mage in play, even as young as it was, I wasn't sure Merlin could win. Plus, we were in the dragon lair, and the other dragons had noticed our standoff.

If I was the only secret weapon, we were *so* screwed.

Merlin raised a magical shield. Before Brigid came around, the Fae had no idea about wards, when everyone was magical, there wasn't a point, but Merlin had learned from her. The dragon mage blasted Merlin with blue fireballs. All dragons could breathe fire, but it was regular fire. This was different. The sand around Merlin turned to glass, and Merlin's face looked pained.

Luckily, no one was looking at me. I pulled out another shadow ball and concealed myself. I stood zero chance against magic wielders. I might be able to sneak up and poke Mordred with my sword, but he'd just have his dragon eat me. No, my best bet was to get the dragons to deal with their own problems, and that meant I needed their queen. I took a deep breath and jogged to the hoard. I prayed all those Fae court lessons Brigid had shared with me would come in handy. Dragons tended to just eat what annoyed them. And I was nothing if not tasty.

I looked at the giant magical bowl. I hadn't thought about that. Merlin could levitate himself, but I didn't have that skill, and the sides were slick as glass. I tested them. How did I get the attention of dragons when they were so far above me and so big? I'd look like an ant to them.

My camouflage had mostly worn off from my run, but I'd made it through the middle cave safely. I wanted the attention of *these* dragons, the elders and the queen. It was their job to control the others.

I jumped up and down and yelled, but I was just too far away. I looked around for something, anything that I could use to make noise.

Fireball. That might work. I dug in my pocket and pulled one out. Then I threw it with all my might, aiming above the bowl. When it was near the edge I said the word, *ignite*, and it flared brightly.

Ten dragon heads turned towards the blast. The top rim of the bowl even melted a little, oops. But they finally spotted me.

"I must speak to your queen!" I shouted once I had their attention. A huge amethyst colored dragon launched from a perch on the bowl and after three wing beats, dove at me. I had the intense urge to run, but I stood my ground.

Mage, do you dare threaten us? The dragon's voice hissed out, its mind voice blasting me almost painfully.

"I am a friend to dragons! Aurora Golden Scales sent me to speak with you!"

I sure hoped that didn't come back to bite me. The dragon drew back, startled.

"I must speak to your queen. It is urgent!"

The dragon bugled. The others around the bowl answered. I looked nervously over my shoulder, but the dragons in the other chamber must be involved in the fight.

"Someone enslaved your dragon mage and is using them for their own agenda!"

That got my amethyst dragon's attention. He looked over to the queen, and silent communication must have occurred, because she spread her massive wings and launched herself our way. If I wasn't so terrified, I'd have breathed a sigh of relief.

She landed her huge self next to the amethyst dragon and lowered her massive head to me. *Who are you and what nonsense are you spreading?* A twist of smoke came from her nostrils, and I swallowed hard.

I gave my best Fae court bow. "I am Megan Findlay. I am Red Goch's rider from the Alaska Sunder. I'm here because a powerful artifact was stolen from the clan—Merlin's Golden Collar. It has a secret function, that of a slave maker, and it is currently being used against your dragon mage!"

The queen raised her muzzle and sent a stream of orange fire to light up the cavern.

She was angry. Her teeth were bared in a snarl, and I took an involuntary step back. Then I made myself freeze. One thing I'd learned from Mr. Mittens—never retreat from a predator. They *might* still eat you, but if you ran, they were *definitely* going to.

The great golden head lowered to me, and her yellow eye narrowed to a slit. *Who would dare?!*

Now what did I do? If I named Mordred, she could retaliate against me—another two-legged. If I named Big Red, she might retaliate because I dared to blame a dragon.

But I'd been raised to tell the truth—the truth will set you free and all that jazz. So, I closed my eyes and went for it.

"That big red dragon placed the collar on the mage, and his rider, Mordred, is behind the plot."

The queen reared back as though I'd struck her.

She raised her wings, then held them back half furled. She started to march towards the cavern entrance, and I hurried out of her way.

The amethyst dragon threw me a look as she passed. *You'd better be correct little mage.* Then he followed.

The other dragons guarding the hoard took to the air and dove through the opening, and I followed them, still confused why the dragons thought I was a mage. It had to be the fireball I'd thrown.

Merlin was where I'd left him, still holding his own, but by the skin of his teeth. He looked haggard, and his clothing was scorched. The dragon mage and Mordred were still hurling magic at him—spells of all colors that did who knew what. Big Red attacked with teeth and claws, but Merlin's barrier seemed to be holding, although it was iffy if he was getting scorched. He probably wasn't going to be able to hold out much longer.

I tried to make my way to him to help in whatever little way I could. I didn't have anything but borrowed magic, but I did have a big sword. However, I'd barely cleared the entrance to this cavern, when the queen's bugle caused everyone to stop and turn to her.

Enfys, show yourself!

The crowd of dragons parted to show the small dragon mage.

It did not obey the queen or turn to face her. She roared in rage.

Dewi! You will release her now!

Big Red, apparently named Dewi, turned his head to face his queen. *What do you mean, my mate?*

Mate? Oh, good lord. We were going to die.

CHAPTER

TWELVE

Merlin took the opportunity to get out of the line of fire, while the dragons faced the queen. We both skirted the dragons until we were standing next to each other. He reached out a hand, and I grasped it. We might be enemies, but we were in this together.

The female mage told me that you used the Golden Collar of Merlin to enslave my dragon mage. You will remove it now! She punctuated that with a roar, all the dragons in the clan flinched and sank down. Except Dewi, the dumbass stood his ground.

I will not, it is time the dragons were ruled by the strongest and largest. He puffed himself up. Mordred stood next to him, a stern look on his face as the three faced her.

Merlin staggered, and I grabbed him. "Are you injured?"

"Some minor burns, mostly I'm exhausted. I need a moment to recharge from the link to Faerie. You showed up in the nick of time." He didn't go so far as to thank me—the words would probably have choked him.

"You're welcome." I grunted sarcastically as I slung his

arm around me and bore some of his weight. He looked like he should be in a hospital bed, but who was I to argue with the dickhead?

"As soon as I can, I need to get that collar off the little dragon. She is too powerful for the queen to fight alone. We can't let them take over this clan, it'd be war."

I got the stakes. I'd read the Arthurian stories and myths about Mordred, who was downright evil. Add in a powerful dragon mage and a huge, angry red dragon, plus recruits from the entire clan? They would be free to take over whatever and wherever they wished. We had to stop them. Now.

"Their focus is on the queen right now, I could camouflage us, and we can sneak over, if you can walk." I eyed Merlin dubiously.

"I need a minute," he grunted.

Dewi and the queen were face to face, spouting insults at each other.

"I don't think we have one."

Sure enough, insult time was over, and Dewi took a swipe at the queen with his wing and with a joint scream, they launched off the ground, screeching and rolling in the air, tearing at each other with their talons and teeth. Both were huge creatures, although the big red had the advantage of horns.

A few brave dragons rose from the ground in an attempt to defend their queen but strikes from Mordred and the dragon mage kept them from tearing Dewi off her.

"We gotta go now," I said urgently. Now or never. If we left it any longer, we'd be too late.

I activated another shadow ball, then dug deep and supported Merlin as we limped through the dragons towards the young mage.

At the halfway point, Merlin staggered away from me, although he still clutched my hand so we wouldn't be separated. He was able to walk on his own again. We gradually gained speed as his magic replenished and with it his strength.

Our camouflage started to fade, so I reached in my pocket to grab another shadow magic ball. Only problem? I didn't have another. I swore softly.

Ten feet further, and we were exposed. Luckily, Mordred was still focused on the dragon battle, which wasn't going well for the queen. She had to fight Dewi, and the dragon mage was throwing magic at her at the same time, weakening and injuring her.

Merlin looked at me. "I'm going to take out Mordred, then go to the dragon mage, wait here."

He started forward. Completely dismissing me. I bet he never dismissed Arthur because *he* was human. I pulled Excalibur and an ice ball out of my pocket. I activated my sword with my magic words, "It's just a flesh wound," and the sword sprang into my grip. I angrily marched behind Merlin, still fuming at being so easily dismissed by him *and* Mordred. I had a freaking magical sword, why would *no one* take me seriously? Merlin drew his arm back to fling some spell or other at his opponent.

That's when Mordred turned and saw us. His eyes widened, and he threw a concentrated stream of air at Merlin, knocking him to the side. Merlin was still fatigued and struggled to get back to his feet.

Mordred jumped off his rock and approached. He also had a sword. I gulped. I was a decent swordswoman, but this was a former knight of the round table, and he had a lot more time to perfect his sword mastery. However, I was a middle-aged woman with a *lot* of built-up rage.

Merlin stood and swayed, and Mordred struck out with his sword.

I had no choice but to step up. I met his blow with Excalibur. The force of his thrust was so strong, it numbed my hand, and I almost dropped my blade. Luckily, the sheath magic kicked in, and my hand healed. I stepped into the next blow and swung the sword at him. He met it easily. I murmured a word and Excalibur burst into flames. That got Mordred's attention, and he looked at my sword.

"Excalibur." Then his smile hardened, and his gaze turned to ice. "It will be mine!" he roared.

He pressed forward, driving me back. There was no way I could fight a swordsman who was bigger, stronger, and better trained than I was, not with skill alone. It was a sure way to get dead. So, it was time to cheat a little or change the rules of the game. I threw the ice ball at him.

He didn't expect magic from a wimpy little human. He instantly froze with his sword raised to strike.

"You mages are just too full of yourselves." I took the time to flick his nose as I ran past.

Merlin rushed towards the dragon mage. I figured I might as well use all of the ice balls, so I tossed one at the little dragon as well. Three minutes for dragons, right?

Maybe for regular dragons, but it only lasted about thirty seconds for Enfys. Luckily, it was long enough for Merlin to reach her. I watched the collar expand, and Merlin levitated it off the dragon's neck and head.

I breathed a sigh of relief. Dewi and the queen still fought, but now the queen didn't have to avoid Mordred and Enfys's magic as well. The other dragons were able to pull Dewi off of the queen and subdue him by sheer numbers.

Merlin shrunk the collar and put it on himself. Probably

the safest place for it, since you couldn't enslave yourself, and that way, only he could remove it.

Mordred remained frozen. I didn't know how long that would last on a Fae mage, but longer than three minutes was my guess.

Enfys shook herself, then looked at Merlin in wonder. *You freed me!*

Merlin acknowledged her, giving an awkward, wounded version of a courtly bow. "I did indeed, my dear mage."

She dipped her head. *I owe you a debt, enchanter, thank you.*

"You owe me nothing. It was an object I created. I'm very sorry it was used against you. It belongs to the Alaskan dragons and was never intended to be used to enslave one such as you."

Still, if you need me, I will come.

Merlin bowed deeply again, a little smoother than before.

I collapsed my sword back into a ball and placed it in my pocket. Enfys's eyes slid to me. I took an involuntary step back. I'd attacked her. I wasn't sure she'd be grateful to me.

I also owe you a debt of gratitude. I could not stop attacking my queen which brought me great distress. Thank you for your quick thinking.

I gave her an awkward curtsy, not knowing what else to do.

The queen chose that moment to land next to Enfys. I jumped, surprised. She was wounded, deep talon marks scored her scaled hide, and she bled copiously. But she held her head high.

Forgive me, my queen! Enfys said and bowed deeply before the queen. She let out a bugle of distress.

Rise, my mage. You are not at fault. These strangers have explained the circumstances.

I glanced at Merlin. She'd called us strangers, maybe no one but Big Red remembered Merlin and whatever stupid thing he'd done that got him in trouble with the Irish dragons the first time.

A silver glow drifted from the mage to the queen, and her wounds closed. *Thank you, Enfys.*

That was impressive. Healing was a rare skill. The queen turned to us. *You are to be named friends to the dragons of Ireland. Thank you for your assistance.*

Then she turned to Dewi. The big red dragon was flailing around, only sheer numbers kept him subdued.

Her mental voice was ice. *You are banished from this sunder. If you are seen by any of the dragons of this clan, your life is forfeit. Any claims to the hoard are revoked, and our mating bond is from this moment ended.*

He cried out as though in pain. So, the mating bond might be more than just a signature on a piece of paper, because with her decree, the queen also flinched.

She turned her tail to him and pronounced one more word. *Begone.*

The dragons released him. He ran towards the exit and spread his wings. Soon enough, he was gone. He left Mordred behind. I turned to look at Mordred, as did the queen.

He was free of the ice. In fact, he was scrambling back up the rock where he'd been when he was fighting with Merlin.

You are also from this moment forth an enemy of dragons. Your life is forfeit, the queen declared.

She reached forward with her maw opened wide. Mordred flung up an arm, and a wave of smoke surrounded him. When the queen's teeth snapped down, he was gone.

"He can't realm walk!" I exclaimed, looking at Merlin for confirmation.

"No, he cannot," Merlin agreed, frowning.

We rushed to the rock as the queen screamed her frustration.

Merlin looked around. "Runes," he explained grimly.

"What?"

He pointed to the rock, and I saw the white glowing marks around the top. "He made transportation runes on this rock. He could be anywhere now."

"Dammit."

"I believe I've made my enemy more of an enemy," Merlin said simply.

"Probs. But he was a real dick, so I doubt you're that upset about it."

He gave a rare smile. "No. I'm not upset about it; I am worried. Mordred has oftentimes been clever at causing trouble."

"Yeah, I've heard."

The queen spoke silently with Merlin for a moment, then dismissed us and asked us to take the collar far away. We fully intended to.

After gaining permission for Darg and Goch to land on the top of their hill, Merlin used his communication orb and called our dragons. We said our goodbyes and hiked out.

CHAPTER
THIRTEEN

The realm walk home was quiet. Merlin was too tired and wounded for much talking, and I wasn't in a chatty mood.

We walked back to Goch's home and bowed before the queen, Aurora Golden Scales.

"We've been successful, my queen," Merlin said with a bow and presented the collar to her.

What was the reason that our Irish friends stole from us? she asked, but her voice was harsh. She was pissed.

"It was not the Irish dragons, but a rogue with the help of an old enemy, my queen," Merlin answered.

Who?

"Mordred and his dragon mount, Dewi the Red. The Irish dragons have banished them and put a bounty on their heads."

A bounty? I'd missed the mention of one, probably because the Irish queen had spoken to Merlin alone.

She huffed out a trail of smoke. *Good. We will also put their names on the list of the banished and spread the tale far and wide to all dragon clans we are friendly with.*

Merlin bowed again, and I curtsied.

You are free to go, she dismissed us.

We mounted up to travel home. Once we were on the Fae practice planet staging for our last realm walk home, I asked Merlin, "What's that about a bounty?"

He glanced over at me. "They will register one for both Mordred and Dewi with the Guild. They've offered some treasures from the hoard for the death of both of them."

My face must have lit up.

Merlin shook his head at me. "I know what you're thinking, but no. They're too dangerous for someone like you!"

My good mood faded; asshole Merlin was back with a vengeance. *Someone like me?*

"What is that supposed to mean?" I snarled.

"That this bounty is for an old, powerful dragon, and a Fae mage. It's out of your league."

"You think everything is out of my league."

"I'm trying to save you from yourself. You are only human," he said, voice hard.

"Why don't you save your own damned self next time, you arrogant asshole. Screw you, Merlin."

With that, I gave Goch our destination, and we realm walked away.

Seconds later, we were circling above the Guild Hall. I was taking that bounty. I wanted to be first on the list.

Darg appeared next to us.

"*How did he know where we were?*" I asked Goch.

I told him, Megan. I didn't know it was a secret, Goch replied, his tone whiny and apologetic.

I sighed, undone from a great exit by a teenager.

"It's fine, Goch, next time I leave in a huff, though, don't tell anyone where we've gone, okay?"

Sorry, Megan, I won't.

"Megan, don't you dare! You have no idea what you are getting into!" Merlin barked at me.

I seriously considered throwing an ice ball at him, but I might hit Darg by accident. So, I would be the bigger person and ignore him instead. Goch landed in the usual spot on the roof, and I dismounted.

I marched to the roof door and down the stairs to the Guild Hall proper. I searched the boards, nothing was there, so I went directly into the office.

"Has a bounty on Mordred and the dragon Dewi been released?"

The goblin running the show looked up at me in surprise. "It just came through."

"Put me on the list. I want that bounty."

He shook his head. "Sorry, Red Rider, but it's a wide bounty, first to bring in the heads gets the prize."

"Fine." I stormed out. I was going to find that bastard Mordred and his slimy red dragon. I was going to claim that bounty if it was the last thing I did. I had a raging purpose now, and no one was going to get in my way. Not even Merlin, the infamous dumbass enchanter himself.

The end.

*I dedicate this book to the people that have supported and encouraged me along the way. To my
parents, who taught me to read and love sci-fi and fantasy. I wouldn't be anything without you!
To my husband for not getting upset when I'm busy with the books. To my siblings and niece
who read everything! To my fellow FAKAs, thanks for everything! And to all my alpha and beta
and ARC readers. Thank you all!*

PLEASE REVIEW BORROWED MAGIC

Wow!

You finished the book. Thanks for reading it. I appreciate it! Please, please, please consider leaving an honest review. Love it or hate it, authors can only sell books if they get reviews. If I don't sell books, I can't afford cat food. If I can't buy cat food, the little bastards will scavenge my sad, broken body. Then there will be no more books. Look at their terrifying, savage, little faces. They have sunken cheeks and swollen tummies and can't wait to eat me.

Please help by leaving that review!

PLEASE REVIEW BORROWED MAGIC

* * *

BORROWED MAGIC
A SPLINTERED REALMS PREQUEL

NOTE: *This is an unproofed sample.*

CHAPTER 1

My red dragon, Goch, spread his wings and climbed another hundred feet into the bright blue

sky. We had no cloud cover, and it was hard to hide from other flying creatures without it. Our

best bet was to fly high enough we weren't noticed or hit a blind spot in our quarry's vision.

Luckily dragons were the best flyers.

Much better than giant flying chickens.

It wasn't literally a chicken it was a Roc—a big bird straight from myth—but it looked

like a Rhode Island Red from its red comb and wattle to its yellow legs and feet complete with

sixteen inch long spurs. I guess if it had spurs it was male, so I should have called it a rooster not

a chicken, but who cares. I had to bring its rider in regardless. I was bounty hunting and the blue-

skinned troll on its back was my mark.

Rocs were as smart as chickens, but that made it about as guilty as a getaway car, so I

didn't want to hurt it. Our best bet was to grab the rider from its back and zoom away. Only

problem was that Rocs, like chickens, had 300-degree vision. We were only invisible to it in a

very limited blind spot. Thus, we were flying so high, I wished I'd brought an oxygen mask.

I was wearing goggles and newly enchanted flying gear so I was warm enough, but I

really should have thought about a canister of oxygen, dumb.

I was gasping for air. Goch, I can't go higher, can't breathe, I informed my dragon, telepathically.

They stopped looking around, I think they think they lost us, he replied.

Good, next cloud we find, we dive.

Luckily, Rocs couldn't realm walk, and as far as I read about our target, Mr. Troll, neither did he. We could wait patiently for a cloud. Dragons had far greater range as well.

Unfortunately, I didn't account for them heading in for a landing. Shit.

The Roc quickly lost altitude.

Goch, we can't lose this chance, we have to dive!

Goch didn't answer, he just aimed his snout toward the Roc, and pressed his wings to his sides. We plummeted like a stone. The change of altitude made me lightheaded, but I clung to the harness. Even if I passed out, I was secured to Goch with thick ultra-high-molecular-weight polyethylene straps.

I didn't pass out, and soon the thicker air was noticeable, and I could breathe normally again. The Roc didn't notice us until we were almost in striking distance, but then it swerved to the right. Dragons were better flyers, but Rocs, being smaller, were slightly more maneuverable.

Our cover was blown, so Goch didn't bother with subtlety. He banked and went straight at the bird.

It couldn't outclimb us, so it dove. But it was a bird, not a dragon. It made it almost to the trees when Goch caught up and plucked the troll from the saddle with his talons. Goch bugled in satisfaction, and we glided over the trees as the Roc continued down to land.

I signaled Goch, and he realm walked to Faerie.

I felt a flash of pain through my telepathic link with my dragon, and he roared in

response. The troll has a sword, he complained.

This is our chance to try the Kobayashi Maru move, I said to my dragon. It was

something I'd thought up for when Goch was in trouble. In Star Trek, the Kobayashi Maru was

supposed to be the unwinnable test—I fancied myself to be like Captain Kirk, he cheated and

won. I didn't believe in losing either.

I attached the safety strap to Goch's harness and my harness, then I unhitched myself

from the saddle and gave Goch the signal. He beat his wings hard, then spread them wide to

glide. He gave a quarter turn on his side. It made us drop faster, but it gave me a stable platform

to perform the maneuver.

I slid down his side and leapt free. At the same time Goch rolled to his other side, giving

me enough swing that I had serious momentum. Aiming for the troll with my steel-toe combat

boots outstretched, I kicked the sword out of his taloned hand. Then I used the rest of the swing

to travel under Goch to his other side and clamber up the harness back to my seat. I snapped back

in and pulled the swing strap up and shoved it back into the carrying bag on the harness.

"A success!" I yelled out loud, although the wind tore it away.

Goch roared in glee at the same time. I patted his back with my gloved hand. I hope the sword fell far away from anyone. Oops, hadn't thought that through.

It wasn't much further to the Bounty Hunter's Guild, so Goch and I took a leisurely flight and landed gently on the roof. The troll was a little worse for wear, my trick had broken his wrist, and Goch had dropped it a few feet before landing, so it was struggling to get its breath as I approached. The bounty called for it to be alive, it didn't say it had to be in perfect health.

I might have felt bad if it wasn't for the fact the troll had been kidnapping other bounty hunters and ransoming them back to the Guild after roughing them up. After the first kidnapping, the bounty had soared in price. The Guild had a reputation, and it wasn't amused. After the third kidnapping, they almost switched the bounty to "dead or alive" so Mr. Troll had better be happy I found him first.

All the fight was out of the troll, so it didn't take much to encourage him down the stairs to the holding cells other than a single little prick from Excalibur, my magic sword. Yes, that magic sword. I didn't even need handcuffs.

The warden gave me a receipt after he verified the identity of our troublemaker, and I went to get paid. I dropped off the receipt with the cashier, and they deposited a hefty sum in Fae gold into my account. The smaller bounties were normally paid in silver, so I gave a little fist pump at the amount. I had a tidy little nest egg growing in my Fae bank account.

I went to check the boards before I met Goch on the roof. The central bounty that all bounty hunters were itching to fill was the one for the half Fae enchanter, Medraut aka Mordred, and his huge red dragon, Dewi. I felt my lip curl.

I'd had a run-in with Mordred. He and his dragon had stolen the Golden Collar of Merlin.

It was an enchanted collar with a large red gem in the center. Its main purpose was to store Fae magic so it could be used when there was no link to Faerie around, but it had a darker purpose. It had a slave function built into it. If someone were to place it on the neck of some other person or creature, they had absolute power over them.

Dewi had stolen it from Goch's clan in Alaska and used it to enslave a young dragon mage that was part of the Irish dragon clan. Mordred and Dewi's purpose, far as we could tell, was to use the dragon's power to take over the clan, and next to enslave the country, and eventually the world.

Merlin, yes, that Merlin, had discouraged Mordred, way back in Arthur's time, and set his plans back until recently.

Now, I was raking the splinters in attempts to find any word of the two, any sign of where they were. It was my driving purpose. The thing that kept me going since I lost Luke.

I pushed that down. I couldn't think of it. I needed to be busy. I raced up the stairs, and Goch and I fell off the roof and flew steadily away.

About the Author

Jilleen Dolbeare is the author of the Shadow Winged Chronicles, an urban fantasy series about a shape-shifting bush pilot in Alaska. And the Splintered Magic Series, about a woman rebuilding her life and learning about magic with the help of her cat.

She loves riding horses, warm ocean beaches, and long walks in the mountains, none of which she can do in the Arctic, so she writes. Her activities are riding her four-wheeler on cold ocean beaches (often frozen or covered with ice), and long walks to and from work when it's 40 below—in the dark. She does keep her stakes sharp for those vamps that show up during the 67 days of night.

Jilleen lives with her husband and two hungry cats in Alaska where she also discovered her love and admiration of the Inupiaq people and their folklore.

Piper's Logbook

Also by Jilleen Dolbeare

Shadow Winged Chronicles:

Shadow Lair: Book .5

Shadow Winged: Book 1

Shadow Wolf: Book 1.5

Shadow Strife: Book 2

Shadow Witch: Book 2.5

Shadow War: Book 3

Splintered Magic Series:

Splinter Cat: Book .5

Splintered Magic: Book 1

Splintered Veil: Book 2

Splintered Fate: Book 3

Splintered Haven: Book 4

Splintered Secret: Book 5

Splintered Destiny: Book 6

Splintered Realms Series:

Borrowed Magic: Book .5

Borrowed Amulet: Book 1*

Borrowed Chaos: Book 2*

The Portlock Paranormal Detective Series:

(With Heather G. Harris)

The Vampire and the Case of her Dastardly Death: Book .5
The Vampire and the Case of the Wayward Werewolf: Book 1
The Vampire and the Case of the Secretive Siren: Book 2
The Vampire and the Case of the Baleful Banshee: Book 3
The Vampire and the Case of the Cursed Canine: Book 4
The Vampire and the Case of the Perilous Poltergeist: Book 5*
The Vampire and the Case of the Hellacious Hag: Book 6*

*Forthcoming

* * *

www.ingramcontent.com/pod-product-compliance
Lightning Source LLC
LaVergne TN
LVHW041711060526
838201LV00043B/679